The Camera

Valentina Church

For Emlyn E. Evans,
an inspirational English teacher

Alice has been tense and uneasy since waking this morning and entering the shadowy alley has heightened those feelings. Normally, she's not bothered by the musty cellar smells which ooze out of metal grilles dotted along the walls, but today she finds them unsettling. Why is she feeling like this in the one place where she only ever experiences joy and a wonderful sense of peace? It has to be the dream she had last night. All she can remember about it is that she'd been smiling into the lens of a camera held by a boyfriend she'd had at university. Things hadn't ended well and she hadn't thought of him in years...

Thankfully, she quickly emerges from the alley which leads into Campo Santa Margherita. The cafes and restaurants lining the square are alive with chatter as Venetians and tourists enjoy a pre-dinner aperitivo. She manages to find an empty table and, thankfully, a waiter approaches her almost immediately. Despite the current obsession with Aperol Spritz, she orders the best aperitivo, a Campari Soda. A glass of the gorgeous dark red liquid, decorated with a slice of orange, soon arrives; the first sip is always the best and she relaxes as she savours its cold, bitter aftertaste. As is the local custom, her drink is accompanied by a couple of complimentary dishes of *cicchetti*, small Venetian snacks. One of the best ways to spend an evening in Venice is to go on a *bacaro* crawl, moving from bar to bar, drinking wine or glasses of *spritz* and eating these delicious little bites of food. It's a cheap way to eat out and a far more authentic experience for anyone visiting Venice than being sucked into a tourist trap trattoria, eating mediocre food and getting a shock when the bill comes.

Although Venice isn't renowned for its cuisine, there are decent places to eat, if you knew where to go. Her favourite is *Da Gabriella*, away from the crowds, but within easy walking distance of the little apartment she always rents near the Accademia. Looking out over the Giudecca Canal, it serves wonderful food and the staff, which never changes, is welcoming and efficient. In winter she eats in the intimate, traditionally decorated dining room, but it's in the warmer months that the best experience is to be had because one can enjoy the open air floating restaurant, where tables with starched white linen reward you with one of the best views in Venice. Terracotta pots packed with bright red geraniums decorate the ornamental ironwork and large, square umbrellas shade diners from the heat of the sun. Dinner is wonderful too, with the added bonus of being able to enjoy glorious sunsets over the wide, Giudecca canal.

"*Signora,* another Campari?"

"*No grazie, il conto per favore.*"

"Straight away", he nods in response.

This habit of replying to her in English sometimes annoys her, but, as a linguist herself, Alice understands that others enjoy showing off their own dexterity with languages, too.

She'd fallen in love with Italy on family holidays during her teens and had decided then that she wanted to learn Italian. Her parents had indulged her and arranged lessons with an Italian lady who lived on Turnham Green. Signora Gretti was flamboyant and slightly intimidating, but Alice had fallen in love with her. Entering her house was like being transported back to Italy. Delicious smells seeped out from under the kitchen door and the furniture was beautiful, so different from what filled her own home, most of which was a boring dark brown. Everything in her teacher's house was stylishly modern and had been shipped in from Milan. Mid-century furniture of that quality was super trendy at the moment, fetching hefty prices. What had happened to it all she wonders?

Her reminiscences are interrupted by the waiter returning with the bill, which she pays before beginning her walk back towards the Accademia. As she reaches the porticoed exit from the square, she hears someone running behind her.

"*Signora* you left your bag!"

She turns to see her waiter holding out the green carrier bag she's left behind. After thanking him, Alice waits until he's out of sight before checking that the camera is still there. It is; thank goodness no one else picked it up! Apart from the not inconsiderable sum she paid for it, she can't wait to scrutinize the negatives which had come with the camera. What insights into the previous owner would they give her?

***

When she'd woken that morning she'd had no definite plans on how to fill her day, but, as she ate breakfast, she'd decided to take the waterbus down to Piazzale Roma. From there, she'd transfer to another boat travelling past the

Arsenale and once they reached the northern part of the island she would get off and start the long, leisurely walk through the Ghetto. She loved strolling through this part of the city - it was here the term describing an area where Jews lived originated. It had such a different feel from the rest of the city and was full of the interesting narrow little streets, known locally as *calle*, which were fun to explore.

People often spoke of the impossible crowds in Venice and, yes, they were impossible for most of the year around St Mark's Square, the Doge's Palace and the Rialto, but as little as a ten minute stroll would take you to fascinating, quiet little squares where you might find the statue of some noble Venetian and a few stray cats basking peacefully in the sunshine. Sadly, many tourists didn't seem to want to explore the city in depth - perhaps they were on a tight schedule. A touch of "If it's Tuesday, this must be Venice...." It was a pity because, if they explored a little, they would soon find the real Venice.

She'd stopped for a coffee mid-morning. Standing at the counter along with the locals, she ordered an espresso and an almond biscuit. Alice loved pretending to be a *Veneziana*, listening in on the conversations going on around her. This was one of the many traditions of her visits to Venice. She liked traditions. An early start was another. One of her favourite sounds was the chiming of church bells from seven o'clock each morning. They never all seemed to start at precisely the same moment – perhaps there was some Italian Tinkerbell who flitted from *campanile* to *campanile*, tapping each into motion as she passed?

The espresso and almond biscuit had been excellent, but what she'd really fancied was a *fritola*, but they were only available during *Carnevale* in February or March. They filled the windows of all the cake shops and bars then; small, round, fried donuts stuffed with either zabaglione custard, or, her favourite, grappa soaked raisins and pine nuts. Her mouth had watered as she thought of them...

She'd continued her walk, eventually joining the Strada Nova with its clothes and cake shops. Just off this wide, open street she'd stopped at a little *osteria*, historically the sort of place where working men ate. Now, however, *osterie* were *the* places to eat. Her order had been a plate of *sarde in soar*, an old Venetian delicacy; fried sardines layered with cooked sliced white onions, raisins soaked in white wine and vinegar and then left to rest for at least twenty four hours. This, with a slice of grilled polenta and a glass of white Veneto wine, made for an excellent lunch.

She'd sat in the shade of a large umbrella for quite a while, watching the world pass by. It had been an effort to restart the walk, but she was soon rewarded. In the next piazza she'd heard Vivaldi's *Four Seasons* pouring out of a church where musicians were practising for a concert that evening. She'd crept inside and sat quietly in the shadows at the back of the church. How magical to hear the music played in the city of its birth!

By the time the rehearsal was over, Alice had been surprised to find it was already four p.m. and people were returning to work after their afternoon siesta. The loud clatter of a metal shutter being raised had alerted her to a shop being re-opened. Curious to discover what it sold, Alice strolled over to look in the window where a selection of cameras and a number of black and white framed photographs of Venetian scenes were artfully displayed. The photographs were so unusual that Alice had been curious to find out if there were more inside and had pushed open the shop door.

An old fashioned bell had tinkled as she entered and noticed someone sitting at a desk. Alice had asked if there were any more photographs she might look at.

"Yes, of course, we have lots more in a room at the back of the shop."

She had followed the friendly young woman into a large square room which was filled with a soft light. Fine, white muslin curtains defused the full glare of the sun, allowing the framed photographs, which covered two of the walls, to be better appreciated.

"Oh this is amazing! I adore Venice and never tire of seeing beautiful pictures like these. Would you mind if I stayed a while to admire them?"

"Of course not, take your time. Call me if you want any information."

The pictures had been fascinating. Some were of the usual tourist hot spots, but they had been taken by someone with the ability to transform what had become a hackneyed postcard subject into something exciting and new. Others were of hidden corners in deserted squares, of rusting iron work on ancient doors touched by frost, of the forgotten islands and the lagoon in every light and season.

A second wall had featured portraits of every type of face; young, old, some obviously passionately in love, others saddened by life experience. How the photographer had found those faces Alice could not imagine. He, or she, of course, had managed to give the oldest weather beaten face a touching dignity. Oh, and the young people, totally unaware and careless of the fragility of their youthful beauty. Alice had always loved the way Italians appreciated beauty, be it the beautiful lines of a Ferrari, the proportions of a Palladian villa or the loveliness of a young face and body. She would have loved to take all of these pictures home with her, but there wasn't enough room in her little house to give them the space they needed to be appreciated properly. Perhaps she could find a space for a small one?

It was only when she'd turned to walk back into the main body of the shop that she'd noticed the cameras displayed on the other two walls for the first time. She'd wondered why they were not in the main body of the shop, but then realised that they were second hand. As her eyes skimmed over the rows of cameras, she suddenly saw a camera exactly like her father's! Without thinking, she reached out to stroke its tan pigskin case and memories of her childhood flooded over her. Dad had adored his Leica and taken it everywhere with him. The camera had played its part in every Christmas morning, family holiday, walk, and birthday party. When she'd cleared out her parents' home after her mother's death, she'd searched for dad's camera, but had never found it.

Fortunately, the ten photograph albums her mother had compiled over the years were where they'd always been, on the book shelf in the sitting room and were now her most precious possessions. Under each photograph, her mother's beautiful copperplate handwriting noted where and when it had been taken. As an only child of only children Alice had no-one with whom she could have those "do you remember when?" conversations, but thanks to her father's obsession with his camera and her mother's commitment to the photo albums, she could, at least, relive her early life through those photos. She'd picked the camera up and carried it to the counter where the young woman was sorting out some paperwork.

"Ah, you've decided on a camera instead?"

"No, I'd like to buy the print of snow falling on the fishing boats and houses in Burano, but I'd also like to take this camera because it reminds me of the one my father had. He was a very keen amateur photographer, and a good one I have to say. Well, I would say that wouldn't I? I adored him."

"It is a fine camera. I think your father and my grandfather would have enjoyed talking about photography! This shop was important to him because it put bread on the table, but it was photography which was my grandfather's passion. All the prints we sell are of photographs he took - and there are hundreds and hundreds of negatives which I still haven't been able to check or archive."

As she spoke, the young woman had checked the small label dangling from the camera's strap and then opened a large ledger on the far side of the desk.

"Now, let's see if we can find out a bit more about the life of this camera. As well as stocking the best new cameras, grandfather was happy to sell second hand ones, but they had to be of excellent quality! He used to go to the Lost Property sales twice a year to pick up cameras he thought deserved to be re-homed or reunited with their owners. We used to laugh because he would treat those cameras like lost children!" Her tongue had peeped out of the corner of her mouth as she ran her index finger down a column of numbers on the left had side of ledger.

"891, 892, ah, here it is, 893! OK, I can tell you that this camera was bought at a sale in July 1982 and ... that's interesting, there are some negatives to go with it. Grandfather always checked that the cameras he bought were working properly. If there was any film inside, he would develop it. The chemicals in the film deteriorate over time and if it is not stored in cool, dry conditions, poof! It is ruined.

He used to pin a selection of the printed negatives to the canvas of an old, gilded picture frame which he put in the window in the hope that someone passing by might recognise them and come in to retrieve their camera. Grandfather was a romantic at heart and he did have occasional successes in reuniting cameras with their owners, but not in this case, obviously."

She'd smiled and shrugged her shoulders before turning to a wooden filing cabinet behind her and bringing out a box containing small numbered black canisters. She'd soon found the one she was looking for and turned back to Alice with something of a triumphant smile. "Ah, here it is, number 893!"

***

The thick, dark green paper carrier bag, emblazoned in gold with *Foto Castali,* which the waiter has just handed to Alice contains the framed Burano print, the camera and film canister. She can't wait to get back to her little bolthole on the side of a narrow canal, just minutes from the Accademia Bridge. It's on the second floor and she loves it so much that she always books her next stay before leaving Venice. It's perfect, with a small entrance hall leading on to a large open plan sitting and dining room with a small kitchen tucked away in a corner. An open mezzanine houses a large double bed where she always sleeps like a log. The pocket handkerchief terrace allows her to sit outside when she visits in spring or summer, which is such a bonus. It overlooks a medium sized palazzo whose garden is filled with pink and white oleanders, masses of different coloured bougainvillea and a large fig tree.

After placing her purchases on the dining room table, she kicks off her sandals and luxuriates for a few moments as the cool marble floor soothes her aching feet. Then she takes the leftovers she plans to use for supper from the fridge. Three slices of San Daniele ham, and a large ripe tomato which she slices and mixes into the few remaining baby spinach leaves along with some olive oil and balsamic vinegar. After pouring herself the last of the Barbera, she takes her supper outside onto the little terrace and sits back in the cool evening air to enjoy the aerial display visiting swifts put on each evening. Up to twenty of these beautiful little birds swirl and swoop across the roof tops and are a joy to watch. It's as if they are saying "it's a beautiful evening and we're alive, so let's have some fun!" What a wonderful way to unwind at the end of the day - perhaps this is why I sleep so well here, Alice wonders. With the twilight dwindling, the show is over and it's time to wash up, and get ready for bed.

As she washes her face, Alice appraises herself objectively in the bathroom mirror. Her heart shaped face is tanned, and her large grey/blue eyes still have a sparkle. OK, there are a few lines, but, in the end, she decides she isn't doing *too* badly for her age. She shivers when she remembers exactly how old she is, fifty nine last birthday. Her ash blond hair, which she wears in a well cut gamine style suits her. Her fashion icon has always been Audrey Hepburn and she'd adopted Audrey's early years' hair style. In fact, Alice had modelled her whole look on the young Audrey as soon as she was allowed to choose her own clothes. Capri pants, flat shoes, and clean simple lines with a 1960s vibe. And she had stuck with it, by and large.

How she would love to have had Audrey's Givenchy wardrobe! She wasn't as thin as Audrey, and, to be honest wouldn't have wanted to be, but she did keep herself in shape by walking everywhere and keeping a tight rein on what she ate.

***

Although Alice is so passionate about Venice, she's always happy to return to her little house on Strand-On-The-Green in Chiswick, West London. She'd been born only a couple of miles away in Queen Charlotte's Hospital, Hammersmith, and had grown up not far from the hospital. She loved London and always felt sorry for people who had to live anywhere else. Her plan had always been to live at home and enrol at a London university. This was because she adored her parents, and didn't find making friends easy back then, but her parents had pushed hard to convince her to study outside the capital because they thought "it would be the making of her". To keep them happy, she'd eventually agreed to visit three provincial universities, but had quickly decided there was no way she was going to spend three years at either of the first two she visited.

The third had been Bristol. She'd loved Temple Meads, the old Brunel built station her train had pulled into and the long walk up Park Street to the University had been thrilling. It was full of interesting book shops, boutique-type clothes shops and lots of different places to eat.

On her arrival at the university, and not wanting to be noticed, she'd slipped into the lecture hall where the welcome introductory talk was to take place and taken a seat as unobtrusively as possible at the back of the room. About ten minutes after the talk had started, the double doors behind her had burst open and a whirlwind of long blonde hair, trailing red chiffon, and Charlie perfume crash landed beside her. A loud stage whisper followed. "Better late than never!"

Alice had smiled timidly at the new arrival before turning back around and trying to catch up on what the lecturer had just said.

When they'd all been despatched to visit their relevant departments, it turned out that, like Alice, the latecomer was interested in reading modern languages. After a tour of the language labs and a talk about the specifics of the different courses being offered, they'd broken for lunch. Alice had wondered where she should go.

"Hi, I'm Freya Green. Do you fancy pairing up for lunch?"

"Hello. My name's Alice, Alice Thompson. Thanks, that would be fun"

"Why don't we get out of here? I saw a nice wine bar at the top of Park Street, shall we try there?"

It had been a good choice. The food was delicious and reasonably priced. Little had they known then how many times they would do this in the following three years.

Freya was a force of nature with a definite Jerry Hall look. When she spoke though, no southern states drawl emerged, just pure Mancunian. She'd asked lots of questions, so Alice hadn't had the time to feel shy or awkward. Freya just took control and made her laugh. The lunch over, they'd returned to the university for the afternoon session and, when it was over, had exchanged addresses and telephone numbers before setting off for home.

When she'd returned from Bristol, Alice's parents had been relieved to hear that the university was 'OK actually'. They were also interested to learn about the 'amazing' girl Alice had met and whom she was convinced was going to become her best friend. Her prediction had been correct. They'd both achieved the 'A' level grades they needed and, after a year in halls, had found a tiny flat together. Their friendship was still strong, with Alice becoming godmother to Freya's only child, Georgie, whom she adored.

***

Georgie, Freya and Rob have always treated Alice like one of the family and she is excited to be seeing them for the weekend. She and Freya had met Rob at a party in Bristol when they were first year students and he was preparing for his finals. He was a bear of a man; a typical rugger bugger, but the nicest person you could wish to meet. The cliché of the gentle giant certainly applied to him. It was obvious from their first meeting that he and Freya would end up together. His calm reliability was the perfect foil for Freya's over-the-top personality, his optimism perfectly counterbalancing her tendency to catastrophise. And, as if that wasn't enough, they made such a handsome couple, too.

After graduating with a poor second in English Literature (his rugby had always received far more attention than his books), Rob had found a job in Bath with a small family-owned publisher. As the company thrived, he'd been steadily promoted and was now its CEO. After his appointment as chief executive, he'd starting publishing European authors having been convinced by both Freya, who had studied German, and Alice who had opted for Italian, that they would be well received in the UK if only they were made available in translation. Fortunately, their advice had been sound and the company was now the recognised leader in that market. Alice always looked forward to chatting to Rob about the new writers he might have signed up since she had last seen him.

Alice's first job had been in the translation department of a large multinational pharmaceutical company. She'd refined her skills there, but had hated the corporate atmosphere. When she was in her mid twenties, her father had died of a heart attack and four years later, she'd lost her mother to an aggressive form of bone cancer. She'd been devastated and had felt so alone at that point. If it hadn't been for Freya and Rob, she would never have coped.

There'd been no way she could continue to live in the family home, because it was still mortgaged and had to be sold. Freya and Rob had helped with the clearing of the house and had trailed around with her looking at places to rent. When she'd found a little flat over a hairdresser's in Shepherd's Bush, they'd also helped her to move in. Alice was convinced that they'd asked the stylists to keep an eye on her for them, because she was often invited into the shop for a cuppa when they saw her at weekends. They even gave her discounts on haircuts, which she gratefully accepted.

Once the house was sold, she was left with a small lump sum - unlike in the recent past, property prices back then rose very modestly. However, the money had tided her over for the first few months after she'd handed in her notice and whilst she tried to establish herself as a freelancer translator. Word of mouth recommendations had helped her to establish a solid core of clients and, after a few years, she was even able to take holidays, usually to Italy, which she still loved with a passion. It had everything: beautiful seas, mountains, lakes, history, culture, fashion, design, food, wine. There were negatives, too, of course, like the mind-numbing bureaucracy and corruption, but Italians didn't let 'little' things like that deter them from enjoying life to the full and so, whenever she was there, she didn't let them spoil things for her either.

***

The first thing she does when she gets home is to check her emails even though she has let her clients know that she would be away for a week. Thankfully, no unexpected jobs have come in whilst she was in Italy and, as it's late afternoon, it's unlikely that anything will now arrive to interfere with her weekend. If she were honest, she would prefer not to have to pack an overnight bag and set off for Bath first thing in the morning, but she wouldn't miss seeing Rob, Freya and Georgie for the world. Rob's success and innovative ideas had not gone unnoticed, resulting in one of the largest publishers in the country making an offer the owners couldn't refuse and tomorrow night there's to be a big party to celebrate the sale. Rob has been involved in all the negotiations and done everything he can to ensure that those who wanted to continue were kept on and decent redundancy packages were offered to those who didn't. Strangely, he had declined the offer of a place on the board of the new company. Alice doesn't know why and is looking forward to finding out what his plans for the future are.

She isn't hungry. Her appetite closes down when she travels, but what she does need is a good cup of tea. Although she takes tea bags when she goes abroad, the tea never tastes the same as it does at home. She fills the kettle and takes out her large brown and white Denby 1970's tea pot. As the kettle begins to boil, she opens the French windows and, once her tea is ready, takes it outside to her little oasis of green. It's a relief to see all the plants looking healthy; her neighbour has been true to her word and obviously been in to water each day. Terracotta pots and zinc planters are positioned to show off the plants to best effect. Alice has planted low maintenance evergreens and ferns and used clematis, white star jasmine and a couple of old, highly scented, climbing roses to cover the brick walls.

The yard, because that's what it really is, had been paved over before Alice bought the little 1890s terraced house. She's been here twenty years. Its small size doesn't matter because Alice is alone, but she often wonders how on earth families with three or four children had managed, all crammed into such a small area. She'd opened up the ground floor, with the kitchen and eating area at the 'garden' end and a sofa, armchair and her desk at the other. She's always enjoyed interior design. Her style is neither minimal nor cluttered, but a comfortable in-between. Lack of funds has forced her to be creative and she's had tremendous fun buying old pieces and making them her own. Everything, from her tea towels to her sofa, means something special to her and each plays its part in the effect she strives to create. Once the tea pot is empty, she decides it's time for her to go inside and prepare for her trip to Bath.

***

The journey goes well. Alice has never learned to drive as she's always lived in London and has never seen the point. In spite of all the criticisms levelled against it, London Transport does get you there far quicker. The Great Western Railway hasn't let her down today either; her train from Paddington leaves on time and she even manages to find a window seat! She's relaxed and enjoys watching how the sun gobbles up the morning clouds as she whizzes through the countryside.

Georgie meets her at the station and, as always, Alice's heart misses a beat when she sees her goddaughter waving to her from the other side of the barrier. Alice had fallen in love with Georgie from the first moment she'd seen her, two days after she was born. She'd always known that Rob and Freya were bound to produce someone special, but she would never have believed how much she would adore Georgie. Luckily for her, Georgie has always returned her love.

In the early years Alice would make frequent visits to Bath but, when Georgie was old enough to be allowed on the train alone, they would have the most fantastic weekends together, or even whole weeks during the holidays. Visits were made to all the usual London tourist sites, of course, as well as trips to the theatre at Richmond - Georgie loved the Victorian splendour of its ornate auditorium - walks along the river to Kew Gardens and, of course, shopping. The type of shops had changed over the years and now there was usually a trip to Portobello Market, where Georgie could spend hours rummaging through the vintage clothes stalls. Alice didn't complain because she loved doing exactly the same thing.

"Alice, you look fantastic" shouts Georgie as Alice nears the barrier.

"So do you, my darling. I don't know how you manage to be more gorgeous every time I see you!"

"Well, I've got excellent role models in you and mum! Come on, I managed to find a parking spot around the corner, but we've got to be quick. Only ten minutes waiting time's allowed and you know what the traffic wardens are like. I don't want to get a ticket."

Georgie grabs Alice's bag and they manage to get to the car just as a traffic warden is about to take a photograph of the car." We're going, we're going!" she calls out to him as they bundle themselves inside.

"I'll drop you off at mum and dad's and then go back to the flat to get ready. Wagons roll from home at 6 pm. You know what dad's like, always wanting to arrive at least half an hour before anyone else!"

"Well, it's a pretty momentous night for him isn't it? The end of an era. I must say I was surprised he didn't take up their offer of a job - has he said what he intends to do?

"To be honest Alice, I don't know. School's been manic this term. We've had an Ofsted inspection, so were all burning the midnight oil to make sure everything was perfect and then three members of staff were off with quite serious health problems. Because of all that I haven't been able to go over to catch up on everything in detail; it's just been quick catch-ups with mum on the phone. Anyway, how are you? And how was Venice?"

"It was heavenly, as usual, and the week passed in a flash. Can you believe I discovered a new church, well, I mean a church I've never seen before? It's a little jewel of a place which I'll show you when you next come with me. As for the rest, I just enjoyed being there, as I always do!"

"That's good. About tonight, we probably won't be able to have a proper chat because I'll be expected to mingle, but I'm coming over for lunch tomorrow so we can catch up properly then."

"OK, I was hoping to be able to spend a bit of time with

you. Will Mike mind my monopolising you?"

Alice hadn't warmed to Georgie's boyfriend. They'd been seeing each other for about a year and, despite her best efforts, Alice couldn't shake off the feeling he was bad for Georgie. But who was she to judge? She'd made some pretty disastrous choices herself over the years.

"Oh, he's away this weekend so that won't be an issue. OK, here we are. Give mum a kiss for me and tell Dad I'll be back in PLENTY of time!"

Georgie's rather rickety Renault 5 speeds off down the road and before Alice knows it, Freya is at her side, moving in to give Alice one of her all-encompassing hugs.

"It's wonderful to see you, darling, and thank you for traipsing all the way down here straight after coming back from Italy. It wouldn't have been the same without you; after all, you were in at the beginning of everything. Do you remember how we sat in the pub waiting for Rob to come back from the interview for the job? God, it seems a lifetime ago doesn't it? Oh, listen to me gabbling on, you must be gagging for a drink. Tea, coffee or something stronger?"

"Tea, please. I'll have plenty of opportunities for something stronger this evening won't I?"

It's so lovely to see Freya again. Almost forty years of friendship, how could it be that long?

"Rob's decided to take the dogs out for a long walk as we won't be around later."

"How is he and how's he feeling about everything?"

"It might sound strange, Alice, but I don't know how he's feeling. As you can imagine, these last few months have been really full on with all the meetings, negotiations etc. In the beginning, of course, it was important that news of a possible buyout was kept a secret. As you know, Rob's default management style is 'everything out in the open', so he found the secrecy a great strain. Then, of course, there was the reaction of the staff when the news was announced. Understandably, people were fearful for their futures and it took a lot of energy to reassure them and explain what their options were. Thank goodness it's all behind us now. Everyone will be there tonight to say goodbye to the old firm and then, at last, he'll be able to relax. The cruise will do him good and I must say I can't wait."

***

As Georgie had predicted, they arrive at the large country house hotel where the event is to take place well before everyone else. Rob buys them a round of drinks before going off to check on the marquee which has been set up outside. Although he is trying hard not to show it, Alice can tell he isn't looking forward to the evening. However he's feeling inside though, she knows he will put on a good show.

Freya, Alice and Georgie decide to sit whilst they finish their drinks. Alice is interested to hear how Freya's job is going. As an HR manager for a graphics design company in Bath, she always has hilarious stories to tell about the weird things staff get up to during working hours and the outlandish lies on candidates' CVs, which she usually manages to uncover during interviews. Freya is a talented mimic and she soon has them crying with laughter. Just as she's about to launch into yet another story, Rob calls to them to come into the marquee because people are starting to arrive.

It turns out to be a wonderful evening. There is, of course, an element of sadness involved as it's the end of a very special company which has been more like a family than a business concern, but the mountains of food and free-flowing wine help to make the evening a memorable farewell. Rob's speech is perfect; a brief history of the company, peppered with funny, but affectionate anecdotes about staff past and present. After the speeches are over, the band starts to play. They are excellent, pitching the songs perfectly to reflect the years the firm has been in business.

Freya and Alice are amongst the first on the dance floor and stay there for most of the evening.

"God, isn't it marvellous to have the chance to dance? I miss it so much, but where does someone our age go to shake our booty these days?" Freya shouts over the music.

"You're right. The only dancing I do these days is around the kitchen, listening to Radio 2."

Georgie dances with them for a while, but doesn't have her mother's and godmother's stamina. As she walks off the dance floor, she turns and mimes that she's getting a drink. With a little wave, she disappears from view.

Alice leans in towards Freya whilst still managing to do the hand movements to *YMCA*; "Is everything OK with Georgie?"

"I think so; it's just end of term burn out. She's always exhausted at the end of July."

Alice isn't convinced and hopes that she'll be able to have some time alone with Georgie in the morning to reassure herself that all's well.

As they sit in the taxi on the journey home, each of the women makes a point of telling Rob how proud they are of him. "It was a marvellous evening" they keep saying. He acknowledges each of their comments with a smile and replies that he had been glad to have them there with him. By the time they get back home they are all feeling exhausted, so take themselves off to bed.

***

Alice wakes at 6.30 a.m. However late she goes to bed, she always wakes early and is envious of those who can luxuriate in bed in the morning, even after eight hours' sleep. For her it's never been an option. She knows she won't get back to sleep so, rather than lie there and start to worry about all the things she needs to do, she prefers to get up and make a start on them.

She pads over to the window and draws back the curtains. This really is a lovely house; set high on a hill, it was built using the local honey-coloured Bath stone. A large garden dotted with trees, an interesting variety of ornamental shrubs and a large expanse of lawn wraps itself around the house. Rob isn't a gardener, so it suits him perfectly because, apart from annual pruning, there's only the lawn to attend to. One of the reasons he'd been enthusiastic about buying the house about ten years ago was that it would allow him to satisfy a long held dream of owning a sit-on lawn mower. Georgie often said "If dad isn't at work, he's at his happiest cutting the grass!"

Well, he's going to have plenty of time for roaring around on the lawn mower now, Alice thinks to herself as she puts on her dressing gown. She's had it for years and still loves it; the fine cotton fabric is printed to look like an old map of Venice with the canals coloured a delicate shade of eau de nil. For the first time the thought occurs to her that she might have become one dimensional, a Venice bore....

No, she isn't one dimensional! She's set up her own freelance business and manages to make a reasonable living for herself. Despite the shyness which crippled her as a child, she'd decided, when she went to university, to reinvent herself and she had. She'd joined every arts related society and was active in the student union. Her hard work with her studies had resulted in a respectable degree and her determination to have a social life had paid off too. She'd learnt how to make and nurture friendships and, after returning to London, took full advantage of the city's cultural delights. She just happened to adore Venice; is that such a problem? She decides it isn't and goes down to breakfast.

She's surprised to see Rob sitting at the kitchen table, the newspaper and a large mug of tea in front of him. He looks up when he hears her open the door, "I hope I didn't wake you when I came down?"

"No, not at all, I woke up early as I always do. Would you like a top up?"

"No thanks, this is already my third cup. I've let the dogs out into the garden, but they'll soon be scratching on the back door demanding a walk."

"I was so glad to be able to be a part of last night Rob; thank you so much for including me. It truly was a huge success wasn't it?"

After a moment, Rob replies, "Yes, I suppose it was.... Well, I think I'd better round up the dogs before they start barking and wake the girls up. Happy to take you back to the station after lunch by the way, what time's your train?"

"Why don't we see how you're feeling later on? You hardly had a drink last night, which was understandable because of having to give the speech and everything, so why don't you enjoy the bottle of Barolo I brought down; I can easily get a cab."

"Maybe. Right, I must get off. See you later!"

Alice watches him go and then begins to read the front page of the newspaper.

A loud "Morning!" rings out as Freya sweeps through the kitchen door. She can never make a quiet entrance, even at home.

"Hope you slept well, darling. Have you seen Rob? Heard him get up, but then went straight back to sleep. You know what I'm like!" she laughs. "Have you had breakfast yet?"

"I'm fine thanks. I know what your lunches are like, so I'm going to skip breakfast to leave enough room to enjoy it all. It's the only reason I come to see you, you know. Although I love cooking, it's too much of a faff to do a roast *just* for me!"Because Freya knows how much Alice enjoys Sunday lunch, she's agreed to cook one today as her friend needs to get back to London to catch up on some chores before the working week begins.

"Well, being *'just* me' is totally down to you darling. I can't count the number of chances you've had to get hitched. How many is it by the way?"

"Only two serious proposals; don't exaggerate! Anyway, you snaffled the only really decent man around!"

"Yes I did, didn't I? I'm so glad we went to that party all those years ago."

"What party?" Georgie has surfaced.

"The party in Bristol aeons ago where we met your father" Alice replies.

After spending the next half hour sipping tea and

discussing last night's outfits and dancing, all three begin the prep work necessary for one of Freya's gargantuan lunches. When they've finished, Alice asks if Freya could spare her and Georgie for an hour as she needs some 'goddaughter time".

"Of course! Off you go, but no longer than an hour because you and I haven't had a chance to catch up yet either, Alice!"

She promises they'll be back on time and dashes upstairs to pull on some trousers and a top - she'll shower when they get back. Soon she and Georgie are striding along the footpath which winds its way around the hill and down to the river. Georgie has slid her arm though Alice's and their steps are in sync.

"So, godmother. What's new? Anyone interesting on the scene?" It was a question Georgie had been asking in one form or another since she was a little girl. She'd always been troubled by the fact that Alice didn't have a husband. Her mum had her dad and all her friends' mothers had husbands, so why didn't Alice have one? When she progressed to her teens, the issue was never discussed, but not because she felt sorry for Alice but because she'd decided by then that her godmother was 'cool'. Alice wonders what Georgie's thoughts on her status are now?

Georgie always seems to have had a boyfriend in tow, but nothing serious had ever developed with any of them. Then, she'd met Mike and fallen head over heels for him. Alice couldn't understand why. He was small, weedy, sported a half hearted attempt at a beard and had straggly long hair. Alice had met up with them both in a pub in London whilst they'd been attending a teachers' conference earlier this year. It turned out he was a peripatetic music teacher who lived in Bristol, but came to Georgie's school twice a week. Alice hadn't forgotten the sarcastic remark he'd made about a new photograph of Georgie on her school's website. "Not looking your best in that one, are you darling?" he'd laughed. Worryingly, during her last phone conversation with Freya, Alice had learnt that, for the last two months, Mike had been staying over at Georgie's flat during the week.

She glances over at Georgie as they walk. Although she is twenty five, she looks about eighteen. Her luxuriant long blond hair, inherited from her mother, usually falls in a loose cascade around her face, but today she's twisted it into an simple chignon. Georgie realises she's being appraised and smiles.

"Have I got something on my face?"

"No, I was just thinking how pretty you are."

Why was this beautiful, bright girl wasting herself on that dweeb of a man?

Alice is determined to try to find out what the situation between them is.

"What a pity Mike wasn't able to make it last night."

"Yes. I was hoping he'd be able to come, but his schedule's a bit complicated. He does private music lessons in Bristol at weekends, and he teaches in a high school there on Mondays, Tuesdays, and Fridays, so I only see him when he's here on two days of the week. He's started staying over on those nights recently though, which is great!"

"Yes, it must be fun for you both."

Alice wasn't convinced. Free board and lodging came to mind, not romance.....

***

The rest of the summer whizzes by, probably because Alice is overwhelmed with work. There's been no let up until now, mid October, so she hasn't seen Freya and the rest of the family since the party. Freya had managed to organise a three month sabbatical so that she and Rob could enjoy a four week cruise and spend time visiting friends in Scotland and France. Alice had invited Georgie up to London for a weekend, but there'd always been one commitment or another which had prevented her from coming.

It's been a long and busy week. All her translations have been returned and Alice is looking forward to a large glass of wine and a long bath. All she has left to do before switching off her computer is to send off a quotation for the translation of a brochure about a vineyard in north eastern Italy.

Although, at the beginning of her career, the bulk of her work was for the pharmaceutical industry, she had decided many years ago that she wanted to have other specialist areas of translation. She adored wine, so after spending time researching the subject and its specialist vocabulary, she was able to add it to her portfolio. Translation requests from food companies had followed, as had tourism-related texts. Variety definitely makes her work more interesting.

She had enjoyed translating the brochure. The vineyard concerned is situated in the Collio, a series of hills near the towns of Gorizia and Gradisca, which skirt the Italian/Slovenian border. She's never visited the area, but it sounds fascinating. It had been part of the Austro-Hungarian Empire for many years and was only ceded to Italy after the First World War as a reward to the Italians for fighting on the allied side. The cuisine of the area has been deeply influenced by its past and is very different to that of other Italian regions.

Although she had visited nearby Trieste some years ago, she was unaware of the excellent wines now being grown on the Collio – well, if the brochure is to be believed, they are excellent.

It describes not only the history of the wines, but also features its excellent restaurant (it had received a 5* review from *The Sunday Times*). She would have loved to see the pictures of the vineyards and restaurant, but they'd only sent her the relevant text. As she presses the send button, she hopes that she'll get the job because it would be fun to work on.

Now for that glass of wine. As she removes the stopper from a bottle of Merlot, her mobile rings. It's Georgie.

"Hi sweetie, what a lovely surprise. How are you?"

"I'm OK thanks, what about you?"

"All the better for hearing from you! Any exciting plans for the weekend?"

"Well, that's why I'm ringing Alice, I was wondering if you're free this weekend as I was thinking of possibly coming up to see you."

"Oh that would be fabulous! I've been so busy this week, I haven't made any plans. I'd love to see you. Will you come tonight?"

"Yes. Actually, I'm at the Bath Services on the M4. A bit presumptuous of me I know, but I can easily turn around and go back if that's too soon?"

"Stop talking, turn on the ignition and point the car towards London. The traffic will be heavy once you pass Heathrow, but don't stress, I'll be waiting with a steaming bowl of pasta!"

"Perfect. Thanks, fairy godmother!"

"Fairy godmother", Alice smiles as she remembers that that

was how Georgie used to refer to her that when she was little. The happy memory fades all too quickly as she begins to question the suddenness of Georgie wanting to visit and the flat tone of her voice on the phone. It must be something Mike has done, she decides immediately.

Instead of whipping herself up into a frenzy of anger over what might have happened, she forces herself to do something useful. She'll start by making up the bed. A spare room friends can use when they came up to town is a godsend and Alice has enjoyed making it pretty. She'd wanted to make it as comfortable as possible for her visitors, but her efforts weren't totally altruistic, as she got such pleasure from the whole process.

It's a small room overlooking the garden. She'd painted the walls a shade of soft white which was pretentiously labelled 'Cucumber', but, for once, it was the perfect name because it was the exact colour of the inside of a cucumber, white with the faintest hint of pale green. She'd splashed out and bought two rolls of an *Osborne and Little* wallpaper for the wall behind the bed; pale green branches of white star jasmine on an off-white background. In the summer, when the window is open, the scent of her own white star jasmine fills the room. An old metal day bed, rescued from a skip about twenty five years ago, along with a bamboo bedside table, both painted white, complete the room. Alice smoothes the pale green duvet cover and pillow cases and is pleased with the result.

Back downstairs, Alice pours her glass of wine, chops onions and garlic and lets them soften in the pan. In summer she can pop outside her kitchen door to pick ripe tomatoes from one of her large pots, but tonight she has to make do with tinned tomatoes. Never mind, it will still taste good in an hour or so as long as she adds a teaspoon of sugar, a crushed stock cube, a generous glug of olive oil, and lets it all bubble away along with the fried onions and garlic. Long and slow is always best with sauces. She has fresh bread and some salad bits and there's some chocolate ice cream in the freezer, so they won't go hungry. Still time for a bath and a change of clothes before Georgie arrives.

***

She rushes to the door before the bell can finish chiming and finds herself looking at a blotchy faced Georgie who throws herself into Alice's arms and begins to sob.

"Oh darling, what's wrong? Come in, come in. Now, give me your coat and go and sit on the sofa."

Georgie obeys without saying a word. Alice sits next to her.

"What on earth's happened? Are your parents OK? Has something happened at school?" Georgie shakes her head but continues to cry. I was right, Alice decides with a flash of anger, that boyfriend of hers must have done something to upset her.

"Has something happened with Mike?"

For a moment there's no response, and then Georgie nods.

"OK. Here's a box of tissues. Now, blow your nose; sit back and try to relax. What would you like to drink? Tea, coffee, wine, or something stronger?"

A tiny voice replies "Something stronger please".

By the time Alice returns with a glass of whisky, Georgie's sobs are slightly quieter. Alice can't bear to see her looking so sad. Her eyes are red and puffy; she must have been crying the whole time she was driving up the M4. Thank goodness nothing happened to her.

She takes Georgie's hands in hers. "Would you like to tell me what's upset you?"

"Mike's married".

Alice wants to shriek "the bastard" but, instead, just murmurs "oh no" and waits for Georgie to continue.

"I've been an idiot Alice, I can't believe it... Oh, it's so pathetic, so predictable. I never thought I'd be one of those women who'd be stupid enough to fall for a married man. What a bloody fool I've been."

"So, how did you find out?"

"Well, it's his birthday today and I was determined to make a fuss of him, so last week I suggested I could drive into Bristol after school today and take him out for a special birthday dinner - I'd already booked a table at a new restaurant in Clifton everyone's raving about. Getting a table is SO difficult, but I managed it and was incredibly excited, Alice. I thought we could go back to his place afterwards – I still haven't been there. But when I told him about my plans he wasn't at all enthusiastic and insisted that we celebrate in Bath last night instead. He said it would be more of a treat for him to have some extra time with me in Bath."

"So what happened?"

"Well, I still wanted dinner to be somewhere special, so I booked at the place where we had the company farewell bash. I'd sort of got over the disappointment and left school on time for once so I could go home and get myself ready. I even bought a new dress and put my hair up!

The evening started so well. We bumped into the general manager as we arrived and he remembered me. When I told him we were celebrating Mike's birthday, he arranged for us to have a complimentary bottle of champagne. Wasn't that sweet of him? We had such a lovely time; the food was delicious and, of course, the unexpected fizz was a bonus. The waiter was just serving us coffee when a woman stopped at our table. She smiled at Mike and said 'Hi, fancy bumping into you here! Haven't seen you in ages. Oh yes, now I come to think of it, I seem to remember Sue mentioning something about you working in Bath a couple of days a week.'

She made a point of looking me up and down and before turning to leave, she asked him 'to tell Sue that she'd ring at the weekend to set up a play date for the kids'.

Alice, I felt like someone had kicked me in the stomach. And then I noticed the couple at the next table staring at us - that bloody woman had made certain everyone in the restaurant heard what she had to say. Mike just sat there looking shell-shocked.

Eventually he muttered something about how he could explain everything and made a grab my hand. I told him that no explanation was necessary as I was intelligent enough to work out he was married. I told him that I was leaving and there was no way he was coming back to the flat with me. His only reaction was to ask where he'd sleep that night! I walked out without paying the bill and made damn sure I didn't see him at school today. When school finished I realised I couldn't face going back to the flat or to mum and dad's, so I made for the motorway. I didn't even go home for clothes or a toothbrush!"

Exhausted, she flops limply back into the sofa. "I'm sorry to be so pathetic, Alice."

"Don't be silly. Obviously, I would far rather all this hadn't happened to you, but I'm glad you decided to come here. Now, first things first; we must get some food inside you. Go and have a shower. You'll find underwear in the third drawer of the chest of drawers in my room and pjs and nighties in the bottom drawer. Help yourself to shampoo or anything else you need. By the time you come back down, supper will be on the table. Off you go."

As she warmed the tomato sauce and put together the salad, Alice thought about what Georgie had told her and was furious about what had happened to her darling girl. She'd been right about the swine all along, but that wasn't much of a consolation.

"Georgie! I'm putting the spaghetti in now, so supper will be ready in ten minutes. What would you like to drink, red or white?"

"Red please. I've only just realised I didn't have anything to eat today and I'm starving!"

When Georgie comes down, she's looking a bit more human. She helps herself to the *pasta al pomodoro* and then scoops up some salad from the bowl in the centre of the table. Alice fills their glasses and there's silence as they wind strands of pasta around their forks. Alice has already decided she will wait to see if Georgie wants to tell her anything more.

She doesn't. They speak instead about Georgie's friends, most of whom Alice has met over the years. A couple have stayed on in Bath like her, but others now live in London. A few are still wandering around the world on, post, post, post gap years. Alice has never believed the nonsense about gap years being character building; as far as she's concerned, they are self-indulgent holidays where the young people concerned don't "mix with the locals and learn about alternative cultures" as is alleged, but rather meet up and party with other middle class friends in Bali, say, rather than their home town!

After finishing their meal they take their glasses over to the sofa.

"I'm sorry about turning up unexpectedly like this, Alice, but I knew if I went home to mum and dad there was every possibility Dad would try to find Mike and show him exactly what he thought of him. If he started banging on his door, imagine the effect on his poor wife and kids.... Mind you, there is a part of me that would love dad to give him a bloody nose!" They both giggle as they imagine the scene.

"You must have felt as if you were in a scene of some film, Georgie, with everyone watching and listening to what that awful woman was saying. God, I'm cringing at the thought of it and can fully understand why you needed to get away. You don't need to apologise about coming here. How did you cope with lessons today? It must have been hard."

"It's a bit of a blur to be honest. I think I was just on automatic pilot. I looked pretty rough because I didn't get any sleep, so had to make up a story about a burglar alarm going off at two in the morning and not being able to get back to sleep. Mike must have skulked in the music room for the whole day because I didn't see him, thank God. I'd left his bag in the staff room and it was gone by the end of the day."

Georgie curls her legs under her and takes a few more sips of her wine.

"It all sort of makes sense now. No wonder he had to be in Bristol every weekend. It wasn't because he had lots of private music lessons, it was because the little shit had to be at home with his wife and children!"

"Look, I know this doesn't help at the moment, but you're not the first woman this has happened to and you're certainly not going to be the last. We never think it will happen to us do we? But sometimes it does....."

"Has it happened to you then? Is that why you've never married? I've always wondered about it. All my friends at school were so jealous of my having you as my godmother. They'd talk about you endlessly after you'd been to a play or carol concert. They were always weaving stories about all the lovers you must have in London and the outrageous things you probably got up to. Then, of course, when you came down for the party my uni friends organised for my twentieth birthday, you became the GMILF for all the guys there."

"GMILF?" queried Alice "what on earth does that mean?"

"Well it's usually MILF - mothers I'd like to ... - but they added the G, just for you."

"Oh my goodness, and there was I naively thinking what sweet young men they all were! I have to admit I'm flattered though!" Alice smiles.

They sit quietly for a while, each lost in her own thoughts; when Alice turns to check on Georgie, she's desperately sorry to see the sad little figure next to her. If only there was something she could do to wipe out the hurt Georgie is feeling, but there isn't. All she can do is to listen if she wants to talk and to show her how much she's loved. Eventually, Alice takes control, "Right young lady, I think it's time we got you to bed."

"Yes, you're probably right, I am exhausted. Hope I manage to sleep."

"Of course you will. Everyone who stays says that they have the best sleep ever in that little room. And stay in bed as long as you want in the morning."

Alice lets Georgie make her way upstairs. As she loads the dishwasher, she listens to her goddaughter moving around and finally, when all is quiet, she goes to bed, too.

***

"Morning sweetie, did you manage to sleep?"

"Not really. I think I eventually nodded off at about six o'clock, but I didn't sleep for long. Oh, Alice, what am I going to do? All night I kept being overwhelmed by so many different emotions: rage, sadness, humiliation, but the worst thing was that memories of the lovely times we'd had together kept creeping into my head. How could he do it to me, Alice?"

Large tears start to roll down Georgie's face. It's all Alice can do not to start crying too, but, before that can happen, she takes Georgie in her arms and hugs her. Eventually, the crying stops and her goddaughter pulls away.

"I'd better find some tissues or your top is going to be soaked through!"

"I was beginning to feel a bit soggy, actually! There's a box of tissues in that drawer. Is there any chance you could face some breakfast? I think you should try to eat something."

In the end, she manages to persuade Georgie into having a small portion of scrambled eggs on toast and a couple of cups of tea.

***

"Now, be honest, what would you like to do today? We don't have to do anything if you're not up to it, of course, but if you fancy some fresh air and a diversion we could go up to Chiswick High Road and have a mooch around the shops, or walk along the river, with lunch on me at one of the pubs."

"I think it would be good to go out, Alice. If we stay here I'll just keep going over things and start feeling very sorry for myself again. The High Road sounds good. I don't have a change of clothes though..."

"That's not a problem. Let's see what we can find in my wardrobe for you. Thank goodness you're not 5'10" like your mother."

Georgie follows Alice upstairs; she's forgotten how everything in Alice's wardrobes is neatly arranged by colour and type of clothing. "You're so incredibly organised, Alice - you should see the state of my and mum's wardrobes."

"I know exactly what Freya's like, I used to live with her, don't forget. She used to drive me crazy. Her clothes either littered the floor or were hanging pathetically half on/half off their hangers. I couldn't bear it."

In the end, Georgie chooses a long navy skirt (well mid calf on her) and a heavy navy cotton sweater with the outline of a big white bow knitted into the front. Her feet are bigger than Alice's, but the bronze converse trainers she'd been wearing the day before worked and matched the padded jacket she also had in the back of her car.

She smiles to herself as she gets dressed. Alice has high standards about personal appearance and chooses her clothes with care, even when she's working alone at home.

"Will I do?" she asks Alice, who responds with a double thumbs up.

They link arms as they make their way through the maze of little terraced cottages which make up that part of Strand-On-The-Green. Some of the houses are bigger than Alice's, but are still relatively small. Every property has been gentrified and gleaming 4x4s fight for space on the streets. Georgie can't believe the ridiculous amounts of money these houses go for.

Eventually, they make it onto Chiswick High Road. It has a

good mixture of independent and more familiar shops. You certainly won't go hungry here, there are so many coffee shops and restaurants. They happily browse in book and clothes shops and, although there are lots of nice things on offer, neither buys anything.

Georgie decides that Turnham Green, which leads off the High Road, still looks pretty, but is now in danger of being overrun by estate agents. She's also sad to see that the old Italian ice cream shop, where Alice had bought her so many delicious ice creams when she was young, has gone. It's been replaced by a juice and sushi bar. They stop for lunch at a new cafe where they enjoy chicken and avocado pannini and coffee.

"So, how's work going?" Georgie asks as she finishes her last bite. "Any exciting new translations on the go?"

"Well, actually, I'm hoping to get a job from a new client. It's a brochure translation for a family owned vineyard about two hours drive from Venice. Their wine is beginning to win prizes in international competitions and they also serve the most amazing food in their restaurant. I Googled them; the pictures of the vineyards are beautiful and the restaurant is amazing. All very traditional, with lots of wood. Absolutely gorgeous."

"Maybe, if you get the job, you could pay them a visit the next time you go to Venice?"

"Perhaps, let's see if I get the job first! What next? How about a visit to the antiques and retro shop?"

"You can't keep away can you?" laughs Georgie. "God, the number of times you've dragged me around that place over the years! I used to hate it you know!"

"Yes, but you're grown up now and you like it too, don't you? Go on, admit it!"

"You're right. Come on then."

Georgie has to agree that it is an incredible place, packed with the most amazing furniture, lighting, posters, and ceramics. There are also lots of upcycled industrial items which Georgie particularly likes. Whether you want to furnish your six bedroomed Bedford Park house, or a loft, you'll find exactly what you want here.

"God Alice, I can't believe the prices of things!" Georgie whispers.

"Yes, I know, but this is London. I don't have any room for new pieces, but I still love coming. I don't know where they get their stuff from; house clearances and a good network of pickers probably."

After about forty minutes, they force themselves to say goodbye to the items they lust over and make for home. As they walk, Georgie becomes quiet again. Whilst they'd had the shops as a distraction she had been able to pretend she's OK, but she isn't.

"I'd better give mum a ring when we get back. I promised to pop over tomorrow afternoon, but I've got school work to sort out for Monday, so I won't have time now. They'll wonder why I'm in London, so I might as well be honest with them and get it over and done with."

"I think you're right. They're going to be upset for you, but they would want to know what's happened. How are they both, by the way, and how is your Dad coping with all the time he has on his hands?"

"I haven't seen much of them since they got back from their travels. I know they enjoyed the cruise and visiting their old friends in Scotland and France. Mum's back at work now, of course, and I know that Bill, dad's golfing friend, has been trying to convince him he should join the local golf club. Dad agreed to play a few rounds with Bill, but golf and golf clubs aren't his thing. I hope he finds something to occupy him. Maybe he'll take up life drawing or something!"

They both smile as they imagine Rob's embarrassed outrage if his daughter suggested something so outlandish to him.

When they get back, Georgie goes upstairs to call her parents. Alice hopes that Freya won't feel hurt about Georgie coming to London, instead of going to her and decides to send her friend a text later to reassure her that, considering what has happened, Georgie's OK.

After about twenty minutes Georgie reappears.

"How did it go?"

"OK. I only spoke to mum. She was angry when I told her what had happened and promised to tell dad. She sends her love and says thank you for looking after me.

I've had an idea, Alice. Can I tempt you to an Indian take-away for supper? I've got a sudden urge for onion bhajis, and lamb rogan josh. I'll ring in the order if tell me what you fancy. And don't argue, I insist it's on me!"

Once that is agreed, Georgie has another question.

"I don't suppose you've still got that old DVD of *Dirty Dancing* you used to let me watch when I was about fifteen? I feel the need to wallow and it would be the perfect accompaniment to our take away."

"It should be with the other DVDs. Have a rummage while I go and check if there a still a couple of beers at the back of the fridge."

The beers, along with Patrick Swayze and the curries, provide the perfect distraction for them both as they snuggle together on the sofa.

Georgie sleeps late the following morning and, after a coffee and slice of toast, sets off for home. By the time Alice waves her off, she's almost convinced her goddaughter is going to be fine. Although she's sad to say goodbye, she's incredibly grateful that Georgie had turned to her for support.

***

It's going to be a busy week, so Alice decides she might as well go upstairs and strip the bed straight away, but finds that Georgie has beaten her to it. All she has to do is to retrieve the old lace bedspread she uses to cover the bed between visitors. As she smoothes it over the bed, she notices the lining is fraying slightly. As it will only take a few minutes to repair, she goes to the wooden chest at the top of the stairs which contains her sewing things. When she lifts the lid she's surprised to find the green carrier bag from the camera shop in Venice inside. She'd stuffed it in there before rushing off to Bath. The problem with being super tidy and tucking things away is that you often forget all about them!

Alice smiles as she sits on the top stair and clicks the fastener on the front of the leather case. It looks so familiar. Although it isn't *his* camera, memories of her father suddenly overwhelm her and she's happy to revisit those carefree days. She doesn't know how long she's been sitting there when she remembers the roll of film and, with a mounting sense of excitement, she carefully unrolls it and holds it up to the light.

Every picture seems to be of the same woman. Although she can't make the face out clearly, Alice is fascinated. Who is she? Are she and the photographer married, or are they in the passionate early days of a new romance? Are they on holiday or are they locals? She decides she must take the roll of film to be developed first thing tomorrow.

***

A couple of days later Alice makes her way back to the shop. She can't wait to see the prints. Despite his initial doubts about how well any pictures might turn out because of their age, the man behind the counter beams at her as she walks in.

"We're in luck, they all came out really well!"

She doesn't want to go through the pictures in the shop; it doesn't feel quite right somehow. Instead, she crosses the road and sits on a bench near the statue of William Hogarth. Butterflies fill her stomach as she slides the prints out of their protective envelope.

The woman is beautiful, with long dark hair and large, almond shaped eyes. What defines her though, is her mouth which reminds Alice of Julia Roberts; whether open in a large smile, or closed and in repose, it is captivating. She wears no jewellery and is dressed in what looks like a man's white shirt and a pair of jeans. Who on earth is she and who had taken the photos? She tries to recognise where they might have been taken, but since they are mostly close ups, there are no obvious clues. The photographer certainly seems to have been obsessed with her. What looks like a canal and grassy area features in the background of a few, with most of the rest in a generic piazza which could be anywhere in Italy. The final photograph shows the woman posing in front of a bronze of a seated female figure, but Alice has never seen it before.

The idea that she should try to reunite the camera and photographs with the original owner begins to form in her mind. Is it a ridiculous thing to try to do? It probably is, but she's definitely going to give it a go.

***

Alice's life continues with its usual mixture of work and meeting up with friends. It's funny how her London friends never give up on trying to set her up with men. Whenever they ring to invite her to dinner, she always groans, "Oh no, who's the new man you're feeling sorry for today?" Sometimes they do genuinely just want to see her, but there's often someone bruised and battered from a recent break-up or, even worse, someone still convinced he's God's gift to womankind hovering in the background. Over the years there have been a couple of men whose company she's enjoyed and with whom she's become involved, but, eventually, they had both wanted to formalise their relationship.

She had tried living with someone once; his name had been Stephen and it had lasted about three years. He was adorable and she did love him, but, in the end, she'd left. He needed someone who wanted kids and who would be happy to wait patiently at the end of each day for the sound of his key in the door. Cosy domesticity hadn't appealed to her when she was in her twenties and she feels no different now; she's happier on her own and has found a way of living which suits her.

***

As usual, Alice has been invited to Bath for Christmas. She's spoken to Freya and to Georgie regularly since the break-up with Mike and, thankfully, Georgie seems to have got over it.

Rob doesn't seem to be faring so well though. In the last few weeks Freya has spoken to Alice at length about her concerns. Rob just isn't himself. Immediately after the buy-out he'd been fine because they'd had the cruise and the visits to friends to enjoy, but since then, he's lost his spark. At first, Freya hadn't been too worried and had kept telling herself it was natural. Everyone who suddenly found themselves with no structure to their days after a lifetime of work feels lost, but they adjust. Rob hasn't; well, at least not yet. Alice hopes that she can find out for herself how he really is over Christmas.

Freya had texted that morning to confirm that Rob would pick her up at the station, so she scans the crowd for him as she drags her large case along behind her. It's a nuisance, but it's the only way she could think of to transport the presents she's bought for everyone. When she spots him, she's surprised by the change in his appearance. He's lost quite a lot of weight, but what concerns her most, is his expressionless face. When he spots her, he quickly re-arranges his features into a smile and gives her in one of his usual bear hugs. After picking up her case as if it contained only feathers, he leads her back to the car.

"So, how was the journey? I'm pleased the train was on time. Hope you're not desperate for the loo or a drink because I've got to pick up the turkey from the farm shop before it closes."

"No problem. How are things Rob?"

"Fine, fine, why shouldn't they be, now that I'm a man of leisure?" he laughs, not terribly convincingly. Soon they're sitting around the kitchen table enjoying a cup of tea and some mince pies. Whilst Alice and Freya catch up, Rob sits behind his newspaper. Every so often he reads out bits of the articles he's reading. With a mixture of anger or despair he variously bemoans the lack of jobs for young people, the parlous state of the NHS and the rise in knife crime. After each outburst, Freya looks at Alice and gently shakes her head. This definitely is a different Rob. Her friend hasn't been exaggerating.

The atmosphere lifts when Georgie arrives. Like all children, she adored Christmas but, unusually, has never outgrown her childlike excitement as the big day approaches. She immediately chivvies Rob into helping her unload her car, and instructs him to plug in her phone so that they can enjoy the selection of Christmas songs she's downloaded. Next, she opens the bottle of sherry she's brought and, after a few generous glasses, the girls begin to sing along to *I Wish It Could Be Christmas Every Day*. Sadly, Rob opts to remain hidden behind his newspaper.

After a magnificent and leisurely Christmas lunch, Alice sits back in her chair, "My goodness, that was more than I normally eat in a week; I don't care, though, because it was so delicious."

She forces herself to stand up and announces "I think I'm in need of a walk, otherwise I'll be asleep on the sofa within ten minutes! Would anyone like to join me?"

"I'd rather get all this stuff in the dishwasher if you don't mind, Alice. Perhaps you could keep her company, Rob? Georgie, you'd love to stay here and help me, wouldn't you?" replies Freya.

Georgie does a very amusing impression of a surly teenager as she groans "Why does it *always* have to be me?"

Freya laughs and calls out, "Go on, you two, enjoy your walk. By the time you get back, all this will be cleared away."

Alice and Rob do as they're told. Wearing a pair of Freya's

wellingtons, Alice grabs Rob's arm and they set off for their walk.

"So Rob, how are you?"

"Is this a set up? Has Freya asked you to have a cosy chat with me?" Rob responds tetchily. "I'm OK. I wish Freya would stop fussing. She's constantly suggesting that I try this or that new experience. Bread baking courses, wine appreciation classes, and you'll never guess the last thing she suggested..... pottery classes! Can you see me doing bloody pottery classes?

"Oh, I don't know, with those big hands of yours you'd certainly be a whizz at centring the clay. I'm told it's all a breeze if you're able to do that." Alice laughs. "How about yoga? Or, yes, I know, amateur dramatics! They're always so desperate for men; you'd get all the starring roles."

He ignores her suggestions and for a while they trudge on in silence. After about ten minutes Rob stops walking and turns to Alice, "No, I'm not OK. I have to admit I'm missing work. A lot. When I was rushing from meeting to meeting and chasing authors over deadlines, I'd fantasise about how wonderful it would be to have time to myself and just do nothing. But it's not wonderful at all. I've lost my identity, I feel emasculated and don't know what to do about it."

Alice waits a while before responding. "Rob, it's a feeling most people have when they retire, you know; it's a huge change in anyone's life. I think it can sometimes be harder for men to come to terms with. Women, even those who have always worked full time, have a network of female friends they've built up over the years; a support system of other mums who stepped in to pick the kids up if anyone had a problem at work, or was ill, and these women often become lifelong friends. Look at Freya and her NCT group; most of them are still in touch even though their kids are now in their twenties. And for those, like me, without husbands and families, we've worked at developing and retaining friendships so that we have people with whom we can talk about whatever life throws at us. We always talk to each other if we're going through hard times. I don't suppose any of your friends who've retired have sat over a couple pints with you discussing their sense of loss have they? Have you spoken to them about how you're feeling? I bet you haven't!"

"No, of course not."

"Well, perhaps you should."

With no reply forthcoming from Rob, they turn for home.

"Rob, you're obviously depressed at the moment, but you have to try to find some way of dealing with these feelings. I would hate to see you fall into a full blown clinical depression. You're not the Rob I've known and loved for all these years. I didn't recognise the person on the other side of the table when we got back yesterday. Everything you read out was so full of doom and gloom. That's not like you.

Have you thought of speaking to a counsellor? This feeling of a loss of identity at retirement is common. You're grieving for your old life, for your status as a successful publisher. It's frightening, but I'm sure that speaking to someone might help." Alice didn't believe for one moment Rob would ever consult a counsellor, but she wishes he would.

***

As the New Year progresses, Alice keeps in regular touch with Freya and Georgie. Each of them has been busy with work commitments and whenever she's asked about Rob, the answer is always the same, he still seems depressed. Thankfully, there is some good news; it seems that he has taken up something new. He's started long distance walking. As far as Freya can work out, he leaves the house soon after her each morning and is out for most of the day. Although they've always enjoyed weekend walks as a family, it's usually involved stopping somewhere to enjoy a pub lunch, before ambling back home. This is something different.

"Well, it's better than his sitting in front of the TV and getting fatter by the day, I suppose, Freya."

"Yes, it is, but I find it a bit unnerving. When I ask him about the walk he's done that day it turns out he's often been walking along main roads, so he's not even getting any spiritual uplift from walking through beautiful scenery, he just walks."

"And how is he when he's not walking, when he's at home for instance?

"Well, he's OK. I mean he does any jobs that need doing in the house or garden and he has a meal ready or at least has done the prep for dinner before I get home. He asks me about my day and does his best to pretend to be interested in what's happening, but I can see in his eyes that he's only being polite."

"And is he still physically affectionate?"

"Yes, he is, but he's a deflated version of himself, which I can't bear. I wish I could do something to bring the old Rob back, Alice."

"I can only imagine how helpless you must feel, Freya; I wish I could wave a magic wand and make things right."

***

Winter slowly relaxes its grip on the world and the first crocus and daffodils start to emerge. Each day, after breakfast, Alice wraps an old fleece around her shoulders and goes out into her garden. She remembers how she used to laugh at her parents when she was in her teens as they made their daily plant inspection, thrilled by each new flower's appearance, but now she understands and shares that joy. She loves the optimism of gardening; planting bulbs on a miserable autumnal day in the hopeful expectation of beautiful blossoms in six months' time. This morning, the scent of the miniature narcissi is almost overpowering, but it's cold, so she has to quickly scurry back inside. Taking a cup of tea with her, she makes for her desk and switches on the computer. Might there be some exciting new job awaiting her?

Amongst five unread emails, Alice recognises the name of the vineyard who'd requested a quotation for a brochure a few months ago. They'd thanked her for her quote, but a few days later had informed her that the publication of the brochure was being delayed and promised to get back in touch with her. She's relieved to learn that it hadn't been the brush off she'd imagined; perhaps they now wanted her to do the translation? She clicks on the message.

It begins with an apology for not getting back to her sooner and explains that, just as they had been ready to go ahead, they'd discovered that some land adjoining their vineyard was up for sale. It comprised of a small woodland with eight old peasant homes which had lain empty for a number of years. The land had subsequently been acquired and the houses converted into rentable properties. They were now ready to move forward with an updated brochure and wanted to revamp their website at the same time. Alice is more than happy to quote for both jobs. She likes the sound of what the owners have done and thinks it would be fun to be a part of the re-launch.

A few days later she's thrilled to receive the go-ahead. The text is well written, in an almost poetic prose style which feels right in Italian, but would sound 'overblown' to an English ear. Alice has to find a way to retain the feel of the original in a way which will appeal to the average Brit or American. This is the sort of job she relishes. They haven't sent photographs of the refurbished houses, but she can imagine them from the descriptions she will be translating. They have even decided to build a rustic little osteria and swimming pool on the land! It all sounds idyllic. How on earth had they accomplished so much in such a relatively short time?

She really enjoys working on the brochure and website and is almost sad when it's finished. Her clients are pleased with the result and settle her invoice promptly. If only everyone would do the same, she thinks to herself as she checks her bank account.

***

Alice hadn't expected to hear from the vineyard again, but in the first week of May she returns home one day to find a voicemail message. It turns out to be from Marco Grauner, her contact at the vineyard. He asks if she could telephone him as a matter of urgency, which she does. His English is good, with the slight American lilt which so many young Italians have these days. He explains that his company, along with two other wine producers from the Collio, have booked a stand at an annual international wine fair taking place in London. They'd prepared a brochure specially for the wine fair, with each vineyard featured individually, along with some historical information on the area and ideas of what to do and where to go when visiting the region.

"I suggested using you for the translation of the brochure *Signora*, but the chairman of our group insisted we employ someone he's been using for years. I wish they'd listened to me because we've just heard that these people have let us down. We need to get the brochure translated and the printing done in less than three days. If I send the text to you straight away, could you tell me how quickly you could turn it around? I've already lined up a printer who is an old friend and will work through the night if necessary. Then I'm going to drive our van to London to make sure the brochures get there safely." Pausing for breath at last, he begs, "Please say you can help us!"

"I'll do my best, of course. Email me the text straightaway and I'll get back to you as soon as I've worked out exactly what's involved. If I can do it, I will, I promise."

The copy arrives within minutes. Alice calculates the cost and confirms that she should be able to get the translation back to them by end of business the following day. She'll have to work well into the night, but she doesn't mind. Sometimes she quite enjoys the thrill of tight deadlines; it will feel good to get the wine makers out of trouble.

In the end everything works perfectly. Marco even emails to let her know when he's about to set off for London. She hopes he'll make it in time and in one piece.

Over the next week Alice often wonders how the fair is going for them. She hopes they are having a successful and profitable experience in London; it's one of the best places in the world to showcase 'new' wines and vineyards apparently. On the Saturday morning she's surprised to get a call from Marco.

"*Signora* Alice, hello. I am not disturbing you I hope?"

"Oh, hello Marco, how's it all going?"

"It's gone really well. There's been a lot of interest in our wines. We have made many useful contacts and taken some trial orders. My colleagues and I wanted to thank you for all your help with the brochure and, to show our gratitude, we would like you to accept a selection of our wines. As you know, we are at Olympia and I think you live not far away, no? When the show closes this evening at 6 pm, I would like to bring you the wine; would that be convenient for you?"

"Oh, there's absolutely no need Marco. I was just doing my job."

"We insist. It could all have been a terrible disaster without your help. As you English say, 'you saved our bacon'! I promise I won't disturb your evening; I will just deliver the wine and leave! "

"I would love to taste your wines, Marco, thank you. Have you got my address?"

"Yes I have. Until later then, I look forward to meeting you."

***

Alice spent the afternoon pottering outside. However small a garden is, there's always something to be done. Flowers need dead heading, unsightly weeds which have forced their way up between the paving stones have to be removed, or trailing clematis shoots tied in. She's just started the last job of sweeping the paving stones when the doorbell rings.

Oh no, that can't be Marco already, she thinks to herself as she brushes some soil from her jeans. Rushing to the front door, she checks herself in the hall mirror and quickly slicks on some lipstick - she keeps one in a dish on the hall table, because, without it, she feels invisible. It's her armour against the world.

A bearded young man holding a wooden case of wine is standing on her doorstep, smiling broadly.

"*Buonasera Signora.*"

"*Buonasera,* Marco. That box must be heavy; do come in."

He follows her into the kitchen and places the wooden box, emblazoned with the words *Tenuta Grauner,* carefully on the table, then turns to shake Alice's hand.

"*Moltissimo piacere Signora.*"

"It's a pleasure to meet you too, Marco. Can I offer you a tea or coffee? Or, perhaps we should try one of your wines? And do please call me Alice"

"I'd be delighted to hear what you think of our wines Alice." With a flourish, he retrieves a professional looking corkscrew from his jacket pocket. "I take one with me everywhere!" he smiles.

She watches as he carefully removes the cork and puts it to his nose. Satisfied, he pours a thin stream of the pale, golden liquid into her glass.

"Of course, it should be cooler, but I hope you enjoy it, nevertheless."

Although not generally a fan of white wines, Alice is relieved to discover that she does like it. It suits the pleasant May evening perfectly.

"I know from your brochure that, historically, the best Collio wines are white and I have to say this is truly delicious."

"I'm glad you like it. Our reds are good too though; we've improved their quality greatly over the last ten years; Friuli reds now account for forty per cent of our total production. But you're right, we are most famous for our whites. This one is called Friulano. My father's generation introduced pioneering techniques for winemaking in Italy by quickly getting the juice off the grape skins and taking every measure to avoid oxidation. This is now known worldwide as the Fruili method. Our wines are more expensive than other Italian wines because we have the lowest yields in the country. We prefer to concentrate on quality over quantity.

Your case contains two bottles from each of my colleague's vineyards and a second from our property, a Verduzzo. I'm sorry, Alice, I'm still in exhibition mode! I'll stop now" he says, turning to look out through the French windows.

"What a charming garden. Do you mind if I take a look?"

"Please do; it's my pride and joy, even though it's so small; a garden in London is a huge bonus, whatever its size. Take a seat; I'll just pop this bottle in the fridge."

Alice likes this young man. He seems so at ease in his own skin. Tall, with a good physique, he has dense black, slightly unruly hair which flops over his left eye. He also has a beard. She isn't normally a fan of beards, but his suits him.

Marco smiles, "It's so wonderful to be out in the fresh air. I'm not used to being closed up inside all day". As he speaks, he stretches his long legs out in front of him and takes a deep intake of breath, "I never realised that London air smelt so wonderful!"

Alice can't help laughing, "It doesn't! What you can smell is the jasmine behind you; it does have a gorgeous scent doesn't it?"

As they savour the wine, Marco tells her that the show has gone well for them and that he and his colleagues are very happy with the contacts they've made. The others have agreed to clear the stand and take everything back to the hotel where the van is parked. After that, they're catching the last flight back to Trieste. He will set off in the morning.

Without thinking, Alice hears herself say "You'd be most welcome to have a meal with me tonight if you're all alone."What is she saying? He'll think she's propositioning him! "But you've probably got plans to spend some time enjoying the bright lights of the city..."

"No, no bright lights; my wife, Valeria, would not be pleased! I would far prefer to sit here and relax. Thank you, Alice."

"Good. I'd planned to have some smoked salmon with a salad, would that be OK for you?"

"*Perfetto*! If you don't mind, I would like to ring my wife to find out how the family is and to let her know I'll be leaving London early tomorrow morning."

Alice takes her glass into the kitchen and closes the doors of the French window to give him some privacy. She assembles the salad and arranges the slices of salmon on two of her prettiest plates. She digs out a small blue and white circular tablecloth she's had for years and two of her dark blue napkins. With the folded tablecloth over her shoulder and a loaded tray, she uses her elbow to nudge the glass doors open once Marco has finished his call. He holds the tray for her whilst she sets the table, and tops up their glasses.

They fall into easy conversation. Alice learns that Marco's family has owned their property for many generations; originally, it had been a small mixed farm with a few vines producing wine just for the family. His grandfather had been the one who had decided to go over to making wine full time and he'd made a reasonable enough living. Not only had his father made big changes to the way the wine was produced, he'd also been the one to approach hotels in Milan, Bologna and Rome, eventually persuading them to try these 'unknown' wines. He encouraged other local wine makers to refine their production procedures and now Collio wines were appreciated throughout Italy, too. They had a small following in London, but wanted to sell more, hence their decision to take a stand at the London wine fair.

"Your father is obviously a good businessman. I seem to remember from the brochure that his name's Luca."

"Luca, yes. The vineyard's his life."

"And what about you, Marco, are you as passionate about wine making as your father?"

"Yes I am, but I have other things which are important to me too, my wife and my two beautiful daughters." As he speaks Marco picks up his phone to show Alice his screen saver. Two pretty girls, probably aged about two and four, sit either side of their mother. All three are laughing and waving at the camera. "I'm a lucky man." As it's beginning to get dark, they move inside.

"My father wanted me to go to university, like he did, but I wasn't interested and refused to go. I never particularly enjoyed school and couldn't wait for it to end. That was the only time *papá* has ever been really angry with me. But I was determined. Why should I waste three or four years of my life doing something I'd hate? I'd always wanted to work in the business; I used to spend every holiday visiting *papá,* learning everything I could."

Marco notices a quizzical expression form on Alice's face.

"I should explain. I grew up in Milan with my mother, but saw *papá* regularly. He would come to see me all the time when I was little and, when I got older, I would visit whenever I could and used to love following him around the vineyards. It was all I ever wanted to do.

Papá was happy to have me join the business, but he was determined I should go to university first. We quarrelled and, as soon as High School finished, I persuaded my mother to let me travel to the US."

That explains the American accent, Alice thinks.

"I started off in New York and travelled across to California by bus and train. I loved seeing all the things and places I'd watched on TV and in films so many times. Once I got to the west coast I made my way to the Napa Valley. Although *papá* had introduced new production methods back home, I wanted to learn about New World wines.

When I finally got there, it was just like being back home; the oleanders lining the edges of the roads, the vineyards stretching away into the distance (so much bigger than in Italy though) and the houses, too. The Italians who went to California reproduced the architecture from back home, so it was all very familiar.

My plan was to try to get a job in one of the vineyards, so I put together a list of the Napa Valley vineyards I was going to approach. There was one with a Slovenian name, Kovac. It's quite a common name around Gorizia; because we're right on the border, most families are a mixture of Italian and Slovenian blood. I thought it was worth contacting them first as I might have a better chance of getting a job when they found out where I was from.

I was lucky. It turned out the Kovac family had emigrated in the 1920s from a little village only about five kilometres from us. The owner, Antonio, showed me around and asked me lots of questions about *papá's* business and the types of wines we produced; I suppose he was testing me to see how much I really knew. I must have passed the test because he said he'd give me a try.

I was given a room in a barn where the pickers slept during harvest time and, after a while, the family started to invite me to eat with them every day. That was how I got to know Valeria. She was in college in San Francisco, but came home often and we fell in love.

My visa was only for twelve months and the time to go home soon came. I didn't want to leave Valeria and she didn't want me to leave. I wanted to ask her to marry me, but we were only nineteen and I knew that both our families would oppose our marriage. In the end, I went back to Italy. We kept in touch almost daily - thank God for the internet and Skype! Valeria came to visit in the summer holidays and I went back whenever I could afford it.

My mother and father were kind to Valeria, but they were both convinced that our relationship was just a passing phase. We were determined to prove them wrong and when Valeria finished college, I asked her to marry me. In the end, everyone gave us their blessing and we had a big wedding on the property in California. *Papá, mamma,* my stepfather, Stefano, plus a group of my friends, all travelled over for the ceremony. It was wonderful."

"So, Valeria moved to Italy?"

"Yes, she did. Her plan was to try to get a job at the university in Trieste, but, soon after we got back from our honeymoon, she discovered she was pregnant. It was a bit of a shock, but we were thrilled. I'd always known I wanted children and if it happened sooner than I'd imagined, I didn't mind. My father did raise his eyebrows when I shared the news with him, though."

"Marco, I'm enjoying hearing all about this, but can I offer you anything else to eat or drink?"

"No thank you Alice. The meal was perfect. A coffee would be good."

"*Espresso?*"

"*Grazie.* Alice, it's been so nice to relax here this evening, but do tell me to go if you have plans. Am I boring you with my life story when we've only just met?"

"Not at all. Do go on with your story, it's fascinating. The advantage of having such a small house is that I can make coffee in the kitchen and continue a conversation with someone in the sitting room!" Alice laughs.

"Well, Antonella was born first and then, two years later, Sofia. Valeria settled into living in Italy very well. After all, it's not that different from being at home and she already spoke Italian fluently. I know she misses her parents and her brother, but they do visit regularly. I'm so happy to be with my little girls every day; they bring me so much joy Alice. I've always been determined to be a '*mani su' papá*; how do you say that in English?"

"A hands-on dad."

"Yes. Our story was very different to that of my mother and father. They met in 1987 and had a *follia romantica*, help me again?"

"A romantic fling."

"Yes, a romantic fling. They met when they were both on

holiday in Amalfi and promised to keep in touch when they returned home. *Papá* was twenty eight and *mamma* twenty nine. I was a surprise for them both, as you can imagine! *Mamma* was, and still is, a strong feminist and didn't want to get married, so they came to an arrangement which suited them both. *Papá* made sure he was a presence in my life and was always very generous, so there was never any tension between them.

Mamma was a *professoressa di matematica* in a high school in Milan. Her apartment wasn't far from her parents' house so they, along with her brother and sister, were always around to take care of me whenever she needed help. I also have five cousins, so I was lucky to have lots of family around me, but I did miss my father..."

Marco pauses when Alice returns with the coffee.

"So, how has your father adjusted to having two little girls growing up in the house?"

"Oh, he's the perfect *nonno* and spoils them terribly. Since they were born, there's been a tenderness in him I've never seen before. Please don't get me wrong; he's always been a loving father, but there's been a part of him that was closed off somehow. A sadness is the only way I can describe it. I've asked my mother if she knows what it is, but she always answers that it's just the way he is. He's been like that since she first met him, apparently."

"Has he had any relationships since your mother? Sorry, perhaps I shouldn't be asking such questions."

"It's fine. Yes, there have been a few women, all very nice and all 'suitable', but as soon as things start to get serious, *papá* pulls away. I've always been desperate for him to find someone because, perhaps then, this sadness would disappear."

"I can understand your need to see him truly happy, but perhaps his falling in love isn't the answer; who knows? You mentioned earlier that your stepfather came to your wedding, so your mum's feminism didn't stop her marrying in the end?"

"No, she's still a feminist, but I suppose she finally met the right man. Stefano is easy going and adores her. *Mamma* is the passionate one, very political and a supporter of lost causes. Stefano just smiles, nods and says *'si, cara'*."

Alice wonders what it was about this man Stefano that had made Marco's mother want to give up her independence?

Marco glances at his watch. "I'm sorry Alice, I didn't mean to take up so much of your evening. I'd better get back to the hotel; I need to leave at six tomorrow morning. Thank you so much. This was exactly what I needed after four days at the wine fair!"

As he gets up and makes his way towards the front door, he turns to Alice,

"I'd like to return your hospitality one day. Perhaps during your next trip to Venice you could visit us in Gorizia? Let me know when you're free and I'll come to pick you up. It would be a great pleasure for me to show you around and introduce you to my family."

"Thank you, Marco. Perhaps I'll take you up on that sometime but, in the meantime, I'll make do with thinking of you all every time I enjoy a glass of your wonderful wine! Have a safe journey home."

"*Arrivaderci* and thank you again for such a pleasant evening."
"*Arrivaderci. Buon viaggio.*"

***

It's been a couple of weeks since Alice has last spoken to Freya, so she decides it's time to give her a ring. As it's Saturday morning, she might catch her at home. She's right; Freya answers and sounds delighted to hear from her.

"Hi Alice, how are you? It's ages since we've spoken, isn't it? Sorry I haven't been in touch."

"That's not a problem, I know how busy you are. Can you chat, or are you dashing off to the shops?"

"Actually, I've just made myself a coffee and was about to flick through the newspaper, but I'd much rather talk to you."

"So, first of all, how's Georgie? I will try to catch her sometime this weekend but, in case I don't, fill me in."

"She's OK thanks and over that idiot Mike, thank goodness. The big news is that she's been offered Head of English at her school from September and is full of ideas for lots of exciting projects she wants to set in motion as soon as she starts. I'm sure she'll tell you about them when you speak to her. Apart from that, no other news. She sees her girlfriends some weekends, but there's no new man on the scene yet."

"I'm pleased the school has recognised how talented she is and I'm sure she'll give the English Department a real shake up. I'll invite her up for a weekend to celebrate her promotion."

"She'd enjoy that Alice. She's loves coming up to London to spend time with you."

"And what about Rob. Is he any brighter and has he found something exciting to fill his time?"

"If only. He's still bloody walking. He bought a book about long distance walking a little while ago. So far, he's done coastal walks in Devon and Cornwall and he has plans to do the West Wales Coastal Walk, the Chiltern Way, Offa's Dyke and God know what else. I had hoped that, by now, he'd have found something useful to do. A charity, perhaps, where he could make some sort of a difference and get his old sparkle and drive back. There has been a slight improvement in that he doesn't seem to be in the deep depression he was in a few months ago, but he's still far from being his normal self by any means."

"There has to be something that'll pull him out of this surely? All we have to do is find it."

"Alice, I've exhausted every idea I can think of. All his friends have tried to get him involved in their pet hobbies. One's taken him along to a heritage railway where he works on the engines. Bill's tried, with no success, to get him into golf and someone else, who's involved with the National Trust, took him for a taster day and tried, unsuccessfully to get him to sign up, but nothing's worked."

"Don't get downhearted, Freya, something will turn up."

"I hope you're right. So, what's your news?"

"Nothing world shattering to report from my end. Work's ticking over nicely and I've been to a couple of concerts. Oh yes, and I had dinner with Paul last week."

"That sounds nice; how is he these days?"

"He's fine actually. He's been invited to some charity bash on Saturday and asked me to join him, so I'll be dusting off my little black dress."

"You could do a lot worse than Paul you know. He's been hanging around you for a quite a while now. Your charms might begin to rub off soon...."

"Our arrangement works and I'd prefer things to continue just as they are, thank you Freya!"

"OK, OK. Well, no exciting news from me. No dramas at

work, which makes a change. Oh, darling I've going to have to go; someone's knocking at the front door. We'll speak soon and make some arrangements to meet up. Love you, bye!"

Alice thinks about Rob for a while. It must be difficult for Freya to see her husband so changed.

***

It's 7 a.m. and Alice has been in Venice for two days. She enjoys the routine of raising the internal blinds, flinging open the wooden shutters, and then preparing her cup of tea. Opening the door to the tiny terrace, she takes it outside and enjoys watching the care with which an old lady is watering the garden of the palazzo opposite. Alice hopes that her next door neighbour will remember to water her garden whilst she's away.

It's mid-September and the morning light is exquisite. There's definitely a 'special light' in Venice, which is why, she supposes, painters love it. In September it's especially beautiful, more golden somehow, the searing heat of July and August forgotten. She's excited because today she'll be visiting Marco's vineyard. She remembers how sweet he'd been when he brought her the wine and how happy with his life he seemed. That's the trick isn't it? Knowing what makes you happy.

She'd originally had no intention of taking up Marco's offer to visit his vineyard, but since her arrival in Venice, the idea of seeing the area near the Slovenian border had begun to appeal to her more and more. She'd texted rather than phoned Marco to let him know that she was in Venice and would like to pay the vineyard a visit. That way, it would be less embarrassing for him to put her off if he'd changed his mind about the invitation. She needn't have worried; he phoned her back almost immediately.

She told him she was happy to take the train to Gorizia, but he was adamant, "No, absolutely not; the local trains stop every two minutes and the journey feels like a lifetime. Would Wednesday suit you? I have a commitment first thing in the morning, but I'll be free from eleven, so I'll send a driver for you. It's impossible to find anyone in Piazzale Roma; it's a mad house as you know, so I suggest you take the train over the bridge to Mestre and my driver will be waiting for you outside the station at nine thirty."

***

On Wednesday morning Alice showers and stands in front of the wardrobe deciding what to wear. She always travels light, but the few things she's brought all mix and match to make a few different outfits. This morning she settles on a white, sleeveless dress which will be cool. A lightweight navy jacket and flat suede pumps complete her outfit.

She's in plenty of time, so, rather than take the water bus, she decides to walk to the railway station. The morning tsunami of tourists hasn't arrived yet, so the narrow side streets which crisscross Venice are relatively calm. The station is a relic of the Mussolini era; a white modernist building, wide and low, which Alice has always found very attractive. Arriving in the city by train is thrilling because you emerge to find yourself bang in the middle of Venice with the Grand Canal right there in front of you, just metres away. The ridiculous beauty of this incredible city slaps you in the face before you can harden your heart to its charms.

Every train out of the station stops in Mestre so all Alice has to do is to check the departure board to see which is due to leave first. Venice is connected to the mainland by a long bridge which was opened by Mussolini in 1933. Almost four kilometres long, it gives visitors an exciting first glimpse of the city in the distance and, for those leaving, it affords the opportunity for a long, sad goodbye. Trains, buses and cars whizz across it constantly.

At nine fifteen when Alice emerges from the station, she doesn't expect her driver to be there yet, but she glances at the line of cars parked outside anyway. A few yards away a man is leaning against the side of a silver sports car. He's having an intense telephone conversation, punctuated by energetic arm gestures, which Alice finds amusing. She decides to take a little stroll whilst she waits. As she passes the man on the phone, she admires his car. It's an old Alfa Romeo Spider and is absolutely gorgeous.

"*Buongiorno.*"

Alice tears her eyes from the car and looks up. The man has finished his phone call and is smiling at her.

"*Buongiorno.* What a beautiful car! I've loved Alfa Romeo *Spiders* ever since I saw Rossano Brazzi drive one in a film many years ago."

"Yes, it is beautiful isn't it? It's a 1966 1600 *Spider Duetto.*"

That doesn't mean anything to Alice so she smiles and starts to walk on.

"Excuse me, but are you *Signora* Thompson?"

"Yes, yes I am."

"Oh good. Let me introduce myself, I'm Luca Grauner, Marco's father. He's dealing with a mechanical emergency back at the vineyard and Antonio, who normally picks up our visitors, has had to take his wife to the hospital this morning, so I am his replacement!"

Luca walks around the car to shake hands with her and to open the passenger door. Feeling a little self conscious, Alice concentrates on sliding down into the car as elegantly as she can.

"This isn't my every day car," Luca says as he takes his seat next to her "but today seemed like the perfect opportunity to give her a run. Would it be OK for you if we keep the top down? There is a head scarf in the glove compartment if you would like to protect your hair."

Even though it's short, Alice hates her hair blowing around and is, initially, more than happy to 'channel' *Thelma* and *Louise*. But, what if the scarf is hideous and she ends up looking ridiculous? She needn't have worried; what she finds is a beautiful navy silk square with flashes of red and gold.

As she drapes it around her head and knots the ends behind her neck, she wonders who the scarf belongs to? After discreetly flipping open the vanity mirror as Luca concentrates on driving out onto the main road, she's relieved to discover that she isn't letting T&L down.

"Ready?"

"Yes, I'm ready" she laughs.

They chat as they make their way out of Mestre. Luca complements her on her accentless Italian and asks whether she's been enjoying her stay in Venice. She tells him that she always has a wonderful time and will be sad to be leaving.

Soon, they are on the motorway and once they pick up speed it's too noisy to chat so Alice slips little further down into her red leather seat and enjoys the passing scenery. She makes a mental note to take a photo of the car to show to

Freya when she gets back. She'll be green with envy.

They speed along the flat plain, passing small villages and towns. In the distance, she makes out the snow-capped Dolomites. Alice prefers hill and mountain scenery and will be glad to leave this flat, panorama behind her. The car is incredibly comfortable, with that wonderful smell of old leather. As she looks admiringly around the car, she takes the opportunity to sneak a better look at Luca now that he's concentrating on weaving the car around the many lorries heading for the Slovenian border. Before she'd got into the car, she'd noticed his well cut indigo jeans, soft brown leather moccasins and the way he'd rolled up the sleeves of his pale blue linen shirt. He is tall, but probably a couple of inches shorter than Marco. His only jewellery appears to be a thin, gold rimmed watch with a brown pigskin strap. His hair is closely cropped, which suits him as he has a well shaped head; perhaps he's losing his hair? Alice has never had a problem with bald men; her first teenage crush had been on the Sports Master, Mr Davies, who was, as she and the other girls used to giggle, 'SO manly!"

He senses that she's looking at him and turns towards to her, "*Tutto OK?*"

Alice smiles and nods.

At last, they seem to be leaving the plain behind them. They exit the motorway and are now driving towards small, vine clad hills. It's all very picturesque.

"We should arrive in about ten or twelve minutes" Luca tells her as they drive through a sleepy little town. A short while later he signals left and turns onto a narrower road which winds its way between the hills.

"This is the *Strada del Vino*, the Wine Road of the Collio

district, and it is here that all the producers who came to London with Marco have their vineyards."

It's incredibly peaceful apart from the occasional bang.

"What's that noise? Is someone firing a gun?"

"No" Luca smiles, it's the noise of the machine we use to frighten the birds. By this time in the season the grapes are beginning to sweeten and the birds can't resist them."

"And why are there roses planted at the ends of every row of vines? They're pretty, but there must be a reason for them being there..."

"Yes, there is. Roses and vines suffer from the same type of, oh what's the word? Ah, yes, mildew. The roses are affected sooner than the vines and so, if we spot mildew on them, we know we have to treat the vines immediately with a solution of sulphur or copper sulphate to stop it from spreading."

He turns to her and gives a little shrug, "Well, that's the romantic reason we like to give. They aren't really necessary anymore because we now have high tech methods to catch the first signs of mildew, but, the roses are beautiful, so we keep them anyway!"

Alice likes the compromise, "That sounds like the perfect marriage of tradition and science!"

At that moment she sees a sign for *Tenuta Grauner* and soon they are turning off the road and driving through an old iron gateway. Up ahead on the brow of the hill she can see a solid, old farmhouse which looks as if it's been there for at least a hundred years. Aged, red, curved terracotta tiles cover the roof, the walls are a pleasing shade of pale umber and the large oak front door is open. Flowers fight for space on every window sill.

As they pull up at the front of the house, Marco emerges

holding his youngest daughter in his arms, closely followed by Valeria with Antonella.

"Alice, welcome, welcome. *Ciao papá*. How was the journey, Alice?"

"It was a delight, Marco, and I was honoured to be met by your father in my all time dream car! I felt like a 1960s film star."

"Allow me to introduce you to the rest of the family. This is Sofia."

The pretty little girl smiles up at her.

"And this is Valeria, with Antonella".

"Come on, Antonella, say *ciao* to Alice" Marco whispers to his daughter who is burying her face in her mother's skirt. "I don't why she's suddenly become so shy."

"*Ciao* Antonella. Don't worry, Marco, I know exactly what she's going through. I was desperately shy as a child and have lots of photographs where I'm doing exactly the same thing."

Valeria smiles at Alice and holds out her hand. "Hi, it's a pleasure to meet you. Marco told me how you took pity on him in London and offered him a meal. Please, do come in; you probably need a drink. Did Luca scare you to death in his car?"

"No he didn't; he was the perfect chauffeur."

Valeria leads them into a large, traditional kitchen, with lots of wood and white washed walls. Glass doors to a terrace stand open and Luca is already outside, opening a bottle of white wine. The girls rush outside, whilst the four adults sit at a table already set for lunch. Luca passes each of them a glass and says "Welcome, Alice!"

"Ah, I recognise this, it's the Friulano we drank when you were with me, Marco."

"Yes, it is; well remembered. You'll get a chance to sample some of our other wines with lunch and dinner. You will be able to stay for dinner, I hope?"

"As long as there's a train which gets me back before midnight, that would be lovely. So tell me, Valeria, do you feel at home now you've been here, what, five years? It is beautiful, isn't it? To be honest, I didn't know much about this region until I did my first translation for you."

"Well, I don't know if I could say I feel like a native yet, but I do love it and, after all, it's not that different from being in the Napa Valley. Obviously, I would like to be closer to my mom and pop and my brother, but we do get to see each other at least once a year and there's always Skype, of course!"

There's a Californian upward lilt at the end of Valeria's sentences which Alice finds quite endearing.

"Everything's ready for lunch, I only need to cook the pasta. Could you get a couple of bottles of mineral water from the fridge Marco?"

Once they are alone, Alice smiles at Luca, "You must be so happy to have such a charming daughter-in-law and two gorgeous granddaughters."

Luca pauses before answering. "Yes, Alice, I'm very lucky. I never imagined that my life would turn out like this. I have to admit I was concerned when Marco came back from the US and told me he had met the girl he was going to marry. He was so young and I worried about how an American would fit in here – this is often described as a sleepy, 'forgotten' area. But, as soon as I met her, I understood why my son had fallen in love with her. Now, I can't imagine life without her. She's easy going, understands the world of wine growing and is a great wife and mother."

Their conversation is interrupted by Marco and Valeria who fill the table with plates of *bigoli*. Alice has seen this type of pasta, which is like thick strands of spaghetti, on restaurant menus and in shops, but has never tried them. They are coated in a thick, glossy tomato sauce. After taking the dish of grated parmesan from Valeria and sprinkling some over the *bigoli*, she loads her fork and pronounces them to be "Delicious!" A raffia dish piled with fresh crusty rolls and a large bowl full of the local red, slightly bitter radicchio which Alice loves, sit in the centre of the table.

Fresh glasses of wine are poured, a *Schioppettino* this time. It looks as inviting as the *bigoli* and, after a tentative first sip, Alice decides she likes it almost as much as the *Friulano*. Is she being converted to white wines at last?

They chat about the business which resulted from their attendance at the London wine fair and Marco announces that their wines will soon be appearing on the lists of two of London's five star hotels, as well as a couple of Michelin starred restaurants.

Alice's eyes are drawn to the two little girls. They had been incredibly good during lunch. Antonella had tucked a napkin carefully into the top of her dress and fed herself without spilling even a drop of tomato sauce anywhere. After Valeria had wrapped a tea towel around her little sister's neck, Sofia was allowed to start eating. She had had great fun picking up the *bigoli*, and laughing that they looked like wriggly worms, before popping them in her mouth. Since being allowed to leave the table, they have been playing together in the shade of a peach tree a few yards away. This is all too perfect for words, Alice thinks to herself.

Local cheeses and a bowl of figs and nectarines follow the

main course, accompanied by generous top-ups of the delicious *Grauner* wines.

When they can eat no more and have enjoyed coffee, Marco turns to his father, "Would you be able to give Alice a tour of the property *papa*? I need to make a couple of calls. I hope that's alright with you, Alice?"

"Of course, but I don't want to take up your father's time if he's busy. I'm more than happy to sit here and enjoy the view with Valeria and the girls."

"I have nothing urgent to deal with, Alice; it would be a pleasure. Would you like to see the houses we converted this year? It will only take a few minutes to walk there."

"I'd love to see them as there weren't any photographs in the translation I did for you."

The houses, which were in the style typical of the area, were clustered in a small woodland a little way from the road. Two storied, with red tiled roofs and wooden shutters painted a faded fern green colour, they each had a terrace at the front.

"We decided to keep four of the properties as whole houses for clients with families and to make two apartments out of each of the other two. One of the houses is being prepared for people who are arriving tonight; would you like to see it? As you can see, we decided to retain the rustic style of the past."

On entering the property one found oneself in a large dining room. The walls were a pleasing cream, decorated with a frieze of flowers and greenery about ten inches from the ceiling. An embroidered linen tablecloth covered the wooden table and there were pictures of the surrounding mountains on the walls. There were also two comfortable sofas and a coffee table.

Off the dining room was the old kitchen. The original

cooking area had been left intact; it consisted of a circular brick construction with a central raised fire pit on which to cook. Rising above this was a huge chased metal hood which formed a chimney. It was merely decorative now because a modern Aga type range filled an alcove on one side of the room whilst a large fridge freezer stood in the other. A dishwasher was concealed in a cupboard near to the large old porcelain sink.

The two bedrooms were simple, with large wooden beds, lots of crisp white bed linen, ample hanging space and en suite modern bathrooms containing high-powered showers. Alice understood that people liked *olde worlde* charm in some areas, but preferred all mod cons in others!

"I'm impressed Luca. Would there be any chance of a quick peep at one of the apartments as well?"

He's happy to take her to a house on the edge of the little cluster of homes. From the outside it looks exactly like the one they've just left, but inside it's totally different. The whole area has been opened up, with the exception of the bathroom, and the decor throughout is modern and minimalist. Pale wooden floors act as a foil to the stunning pieces of modern furniture. Light colours are everywhere with the occasional flash of red or purple. What adds to the sense of space is that the rear wall has been removed and replaced with glass. It's a stunning apartment.

"Are the other apartments like this one?"

"The interior spaces are the same and have the same modern feel, but the furniture and colours are individual to each one. Quite a few of the clients we've had this summer have already made bookings for next year, so we are hopeful for the future!

It was Valeria's idea that we should take on this project and I was a little nervous about it in the beginning. But, I had to accept that if I want Marco to take the business over eventually, Valeria has to feel she had some input into their future too."

"That was a wise move, Luca. She's obviously got an interior decorator's eye."

After leaving the apartment, they walk past the pretty swimming pool which nestles into the side of the hill and leave the houses behind as they climb the hill where the vineyards meet the woodland. It's a glorious afternoon. As they walk through the rows of vines, Alice notices Luca's eyes carefully scrutinizing the grapes.

"Are they looking up to standard?" she asks.

"Yes, everything seems to be in order. If we don't have any bad storms before the harvest, we should have a decent vintage this year."

They walk on, threading their way through the vines, until they reach the top of the hill, where they pause to take in the panorama. In the distance Alice notices a medieval looking castle perched on top of a hill, with a town spreading out beneath it. She assumes the town must be Gorizia because she'd read it had a castle. She can't believe how peaceful it is here and it's only at moments like these that one realises how frenetic London is. When you live there you don't notice it; it just becomes the norm.

On their way back towards the farm house they chat about inconsequential things and Alice becomes aware that she's totally relaxed and having a wonderful time. She's enjoying Luca's company; he's charming, and seems to be interested in what she has to say, but, then, he's probably charming to everyone, she tells herself. His mobile rings. It's Marco checking on when they are coming back as he has a proposition for them.

"He won't tell me what they are proposing. He says we will have to wait until we get back" Luca shrugs.

Once they get there, they see Valeria waiting for them at the front door. "So Alice, what do you think of the properties?"

"They're stunning! It's all wonderful; the setting in the little woodland, the pool and what you've done with the interiors is brilliant. I love the traditional houses, of course, but was blown away by those apartments. You've got talent, but you don't need me to tell you that. I understand that some of your visitors have already made repeat bookings for next year!"

"Yeah, it's kind of neat, isn't it?"

Luca turns to Marco, "So what's this proposition?"

"Well, originally Valeria and I thought that we would offer Alice dinner at our restaurant, but there's a *sagra* in Cormons tonight – I'm sure you know all about *sagre*, Alice. The girls have been nagging us to take them along, so we were wondering if you'd both like to join us? They're such fun, Alice; there'll be suckling pig, grilled chicken, local wine and a band!"

"It sounds like fun, Marco, but would I still be able to get the last train?"

"Yes there's a train which leaves at 10 p.m., but Valeria and I have a better idea. Why don't you stay here tonight? We have plenty of room and then you can make your way back to Venice first thing tomorrow."

Alice's first reaction is to say no, but then she realises she has no definite plans for tomorrow, so she agrees to stay the night.

***

Alice obeys the illuminated sign and buckles herself into her seat. For the first time in her life she's glad to be leaving Venice and that feeling makes her sad. The trip to the vineyard had started so well; it had been exciting to see everything and get to know the whole family who had all been so welcoming. She'd been surprised by how much she had enjoyed spending time with Luca; he'd proved to be a fascinating man. And the *sagra* had been an unexpected and magical bonus, of course. But what on earth had happened to make Luca behave so strangely towards her late last night and then again this morning? She's still baffled by the whole thing, despite having lain awake for most of the night trying to work it out. As Venice disappears from view beneath her, she starts to go over the events of the last twenty four hours yet another time.

During their walk around the property she and Luca had seemed relaxed in each other's company and when Marco and Valeria had suggested going to the *sagra*, he'd given the impression that he wanted her stay on, too. And it had been fun.

The little town square was full of families with grandparents, aunts and uncles in tow, all having a wonderful time. Lights in the trees surrounding the square and the little band added to the party atmosphere. A dance floor had been set up and a few older couples were already circling the dance floor to Domenico Modugno's famous hit, *Volare,* as they'd arrived. Some toddlers had joined the dancing and it was sweet to see the older couples laughing as they negotiated their way around them.

The entrance charge included a portion of suckling pig or chicken with sautéed potatoes, half a bottle of red or white wine, a small bottle of mineral water and a nectarine! Trestle tables had been set up in the side streets where you could sit and enjoy your feast.

Once they'd eaten, they had made their way back into the square and spent some time watching the dancers. All human life was there, from couples who looked as if they'd been together for an eternity, to those who were dancing rather tentatively together for possibly the first time. Then there were the elderly grandmothers, dancing sedately bust-to-bust, their husbands long gone, but still determined to enjoy the music.

Alice had suggested that she look after the girls for a while so that Marco and Valeria could have some fun together on the dance floor and asked if she might be allowed to buy them an ice cream. Her offer was eagerly accepted. Luca suggested that they go to a *gelateria* a short distance away as it would be quieter and a little less crowded.

They had sat in the park, enjoying their ice creams, strawberry for the girls, vanilla for Luca and dark chocolate for Alice. When it came to ice creams she was unadventurous. It was always dark chocolate for her because she loved its intense flavour. She used to feel guilty sometimes about not trying other flavours, but had come to the conclusion that she should stick to what she knew she enjoyed.

"It's been such a marvellous day, Luca. Thank you for picking me up this morning and for showing me around. You're very lucky to have this perfect life."

He didn't respond straight away.

"Yes, I know how lucky I am and I thank God, if he exists, for it, but you're an intelligent woman, Alice, and you know that no life is perfect."

In the moments that followed Alice had felt that his thoughts were transporting Luca far away from the park. She would have given anything to know what he was thinking about.

"*Nonno, nonno!*"

Antonella and Sofia had finished their ice creams and suddenly wanted their parents. Back in the square, they'd soon spotted Marco and Valeria who were just leaving the dance floor.

"Thank you, Alice, that was so much fun!" Valeria smiled.

"No problem at all. Dancing is such a joy, isn't it? We enjoyed our ice creams didn't we girls?"

Alice had noticed Marco looking pointedly at his father and discreetly nodding towards the dance floor.

"Don't worry Marco. I was just about to ask Alice to dance."

Luca turned out to be a great dancer, with no inhibitions at all once he'd reached the dance floor. She'd been happy to abandon herself to the music, too, and had told herself to store this wonderful evening in her memory bank.

They had been dancing for about ten minutes when Luca had leant towards her, "I think Marco and Valeria are ready to leave". She'd been sad to leave the *sagra,* but had understood that the girls needed to get to bed. As soon as they got back to the farm house they'd said goodnight to Marco and Valeria and got a brief hug from each of the sleepy little girls.

"Can I offer you a *digestivo* or, perhaps, a whisky Alice?"

"No, thank you, Luca, but I'd love a cup of tea. A camomile if you've got some - I think I need something calming after such an exciting evening!"

"Why don't you go out onto the terrace as it's still warm; I'll bring the drinks out in a moment."

Alice had been happy to sit and enjoy the stillness and the

black velvet sky. It was thrilling to see the stars. Even though there was some light pollution here, so many more stars were visible than back home. It was so quiet too, apart from the comforting sound of the crickets.

"Here we are, *una camomila per la Signora*!"

Luca had brought a tumbler of whisky for himself. "Alice, do you mind if I ask you a personal question?

"No, I don't mind you asking at all, but, first, I have a question for you. This tradition of addressing any woman over thirty as '*Signora*' has always intrigued me. Do you think it's a 'courtesy' of the old patriarchy so that spinsters won't feel too ashamed of their unmarried state?" Alice had laughed.

After a short pause Luca had replied, "I suppose in the old days women were expected to get married. The assumption was that it was all they aspired to, so, perhaps, you are right."

"Did they I wonder? Anyway, what's your question?"

"Is there a *Signor* Thompson?"

"No, there's never has been a *Signor* Thompson. I have been offered the opportunity to become someone's wife a couple of times, but the whole idea has always filled me with dread. I've never regretted my decisions because I value my independence. That doesn't mean that I'm anti-men of course; I enjoy their company enormously! I just wouldn't ever want to be with one 24 hours a day.

My turn now; why isn't there a beautiful *Signora* Grauner at your side?"

He'd waited a while before replying. He was obviously the sort of person who carefully considered any question before giving his answer.

"Alice, I'm sorry for having asked you such a personal question; please believe me, it is not something I normally do, because I value my own privacy greatly. But I did ask and I suppose you do have the right to do the same thing to me.

When I was young I always dreamt of meeting the perfect girl and getting married. My parents married young, as was the tradition then, and were very happy. I remember there wasn't a day when my father didn't tell *mamma* he loved her. My brother Stefano and I used to laugh at them both, always behaving like romantic teenagers, but, deep down, of course, we were proud that they weren't quarrelling like so many of the parents of our friends. I remember so clearly how my mother would always prepare herself for *papá's* return with fresh lipstick and a spritz of cologne. I wanted that for myself too; someone to share my life, someone I could love forever."

"And Marco's mother wasn't that person?"

"No, she wasn't. But she is a remarkable woman and I do love her.

I think I need another whisky; I'm not the type of person who discusses his past, but I've enjoyed today Alice, so will try on this occasion. I'll be back in a moment."

Left alone, Alice had experienced a whole raft of different emotions. She'd enjoyed her time with Luca too. She found him attractive and excellent company. But she had recognised something Marco had mentioned in London, an inner reserve or sadness in his father. Although he was outwardly full of charm and bonhomie, there was definitely an inner restraint. The only time that he'd been different was when he'd been dancing. She'd been wondering what had made him like this, when she heard him making his way back outside.

"Are you going to force me to continue?" he'd asked with a weak laugh.

"Of course not, Luca. Please, let's forget about it; it's late and time to say goodnight, I think. Thank you so much for everything today; you've all been so kind. Do you think it would be possible to call a cab in the morning to take me to the station? Don't forget, you all promised there would be no question of driving me back to Venice if I stayed the night."

"If you're sure about the train, at least allow me to drive you to the station. There's a *rapido* which leaves at eleven, so why don't we meet at nine? That way I can give you a quick tour en route to the station."

Alice had agreed and said goodnight. The bedside light had been on in her bedroom and next to it had stood a bottle of mineral water and some *biscotti*. What a sweet girl Valeria was.

A pretty cotton nightie was spread out on the bed and, alongside there was even a pair of towelling white slippers in a little cellophane packet. She had stepped out of her dress and laid it neatly over the back of an old, carved, wooden chair. She'd been grateful to have the little en suite shower room and loo at her disposal, too, because she hated creeping to the bathroom in someone else's house.

After a good night's sleep Alice had woken early, as usual. She'd looked around the pretty little bedroom and thought about how strange it was that she was there. She was glad that she had accepted the invitation to stay, but now needed to get back to Venice. Her flight was at two thirty tomorrow, so this was her last full day. Foolishly, she had almost felt guilty for having abandoned her favourite city.

She'd wished she had a change of clothes to get into, but her dress seemed to have recovered overnight and didn't look that bad. Valeria had thoughtfully put bottles of cleanser and moisturiser in the shower room, so, with the addition of some mascara and lipstick, Alice had felt ready to go downstairs.

Alice heard the girls' voices before she reached the kitchen. As she walked through the door, they'd rushed towards her shouting, "Aleeeees!" - the English pronunciation of 'Alice' was difficult for them. She'd bent down and given each of them a hug.

"I hope you slept well Alice? Come and have some breakfast. What would you like?" Valeria had asked her.

"Breakfast tea if you have some, please, and perhaps a slice of toast?"

"Sure, no problem. You can try some of the fig preserve I've made. Please give me an honest opinion, as it's the first time I've made it."

"Thanks for the nightie and toiletries; you're a life saver!"

"You're welcome. So, did you enjoy the *sagra*?"

"Oh yes, I had a great time, but I have to admit the best part was to being able to get onto the dance floor. I could have gone on all night!"

"I'm sorry we had to cut the evening short, but the girls needed their beds. It's a pity that we hadn't taken two cars; then you and Luca could have stayed on. Do you know, Alice, in all the years I've been with Marco, I've only seen his dad dance twice and that was at our wedding and yesterday. Luca is the perfect gentlemen so, of course, he did what was expected and danced at his son's wedding, but I can't tell you what a surprise it was to see him enjoying himself and really letting go last night! Marco was happy too; he thinks you're good for his *papá*.'

Alice had felt herself blushing, "Well, that's very sweet of Marco."

"What's very sweet of me?" Marco had asked as he joined them. "Good morning, Alice."

"I was just telling Alice about how happy we were to see your pop dancing."

"Yes, it was a great, but pleasant, surprise."

"Your father was just being gallant – he'd guessed how desperate I was to dance and just did the decent thing. By the way, last night he kindly offered to drive me to the station to catch the rapido to Venice."

"Are you sure you couldn't stay a little longer, Alice?" Valeria had asked, placing a hand on their visitor's arm. "It's been fun to have another woman in the house to chat to."

"No, I'm sorry, I must get back today. I have to pack and I have certain traditions I like to observe – goodness, that sounds a bit weird doesn't it? It's just that I like to take time to say goodbye to all my favourite places..."

"Alice, I'm sorry, but I have to leave now, so I must say goodbye. I've got an appointment in Trieste. Thank you for visiting us. I hope you will visit us again soon."

"Thank you, Marco. And if ever you both fancy a weekend in London, please get in touch. You'd be welcome to stay, of course, if you don't mind squeezing into my little house!"

"That would be great Alice and if Marco is too busy to come with me, maybe I could come for a shopping trip on my own", Valeria had joked.

After a hug and a kiss on the cheek from Marco, he had left, wishing her, "*Arrivedercie buon viaggio!*"

Valeria and Alice had begun to clear the breakfast things.

"Do you know if Luca's up yet?"

"Oh, yes, he was up and out at about six this morning. It's his usual routine, especially at this time of the year. He can't relax until he's checked on the vines. He bought an old 1960s Vespa a couple of years ago and did it up. It's his pride and joy after the Alfa and he now zips around the property on it. Of course, he always finds something he has to check, so we're never quite certain when he'll get back, but don't worry, if he said he'd be here, he will be. What time did he say to meet?"

"Nine."

She'd been right. At just before nine they'd heard the sound of the Vespa.

Luca looked rested and even more handsome than the night before. After scooping his granddaughters up into his arms and kissing them both, he'd turned to Alice

"We should leave now, that way I can honour my promise to give you a quick tour of Gorizia and take you up to the castle you saw yesterday when we were on our walk."

"I'm ready to go. Valeria, it's been very special being here with you all. Thank you very much for all your kindness and hospitality."

She'd waved goodbye to the girls and their mum as Luca began to accelerate away from the house and was surprised by how sorry she'd felt to be leaving them. Her thoughts were interrupted by Luca.

"First, I will show you the river Isonzo. It rises high up in the Julian Alps in Slovenia and flows into the Adriatic. It's famous because it used to be the border between Italy and the old Austro-Hungarian Empire. It was the scene of a series of twelve terrible battles in the First World War but now it's just a beautifully clear mountain river which has the most amazing colour. Here we are."

He'd parked on the side of the road about twenty metres from a road bridge and as they'd walked out over the bridge, she'd looked down at the rushing torrent far below. Luca hadn't exaggerated about the colour; it was the most amazing shade of turquoise.

"Wow, I've never seen a river that colour!"

"It is beautiful isn't it? Would you believe that between the 1920s and the 1950s people used to bathe in this river? My parents used to meet up with their friends here every day in the summer whilst they were at school and even after they left. They'd sit on the rocks to sunbathe and then jump into the icy water. No one had cars in those days. If you had a bicycle and were prepared to slog through the mountains to the beaches at Sistiana, near Trieste, you could get to the sea, but most local people used the Isonzo instead. When I was a boy, I used to beg my parents to let me swim here, too, but they always insisted that it was too dangerous."

"I think they were right. It seems very fast flowing and it must have been a terrible shock to the system after lying in the sun!"

"Yes, and people did die - the currents in the middle are extremely dangerous."

Next, he'd driven her around the sleepy little town and up to the castle. The 360 degree view is impressive, with the Slovenian border nearby. In the middle distance was Nova Gorica, the new town which Tito built after the revised border had been agreed by the Second World War allies. Luca explained that the first castle on that site had been built in the eleventh century, then enlarged in the fifteenth century when the Republic of Venice won this area from the Holy Roman Empire. It had been bombed heavily in the First World War and been rebuilt in the original medieval style in the 1930s. It really did have the feel of a fairy tale castle.

With about forty minutes before the train was due to leave, they had decided to have a coffee in the little open air cafe inside the castle walls. They'd been the only people there. Whilst Luca had been giving her his tour of Gorizia, the awkwardness with which their time together back at the farmhouse had ended last night seemed to have been forgotten, but it suddenly returned. Neither of them seemed to know what to talk about.

Alice had tried frantically to think of something to say, then had remembered the photographs she'd brought to Venice with her. Might Luca be able to suggest where they'd been taken? It was a long shot, but worth a try and at least it would give them something to talk about. Before she'd left London she'd tucked them into the large leather bag she always carried with her on her trips.

"Luca, may I show you some photographs? I'm trying to find out where they were taken. I don't think it's Venice; hang on a minute while I dig them out."

She had rummaged into the bottom of her bag for what had seemed like an eternity before finding them.

"Ah, here they are. Could you take a quick look to see if you can place them?"

It had been obvious that he wasn't over-enthusiastic about looking at some random pictures, but he had taken them from her. She had watched as he looked at the first print and been surprised by a sudden change in his demeanour. He hadn't said a word, but his expression had suddenly hardened. He'd flicked quickly through the rest and then, avoiding eye contact with her, handed the prints back to her.

"I'll pay the bill and take you to the station."

His innate old world courtesy had ensured that he opened the car door for her, but he didn't say a word during the short journey. Feeling totally bewildered by his behaviour, Alice had got out of the car as soon as he'd pulled up in front of the station. He had told her very matter of factly that her train would arrive in about ten minutes, put the car into gear and roared off.

She'd stood there wondering what on earth had happened? It surely couldn't still be because she'd asked him about his marital status last night could it? She'd remembered Marco telling her that his father was a very private person, and yet it had been Luca who had asked the first personal question... If she had offended him, why had he still given her the tour and lift to the station? He could easily have found some excuse and booked a taxi.

By the time the train had pulled into the station, she'd decided that she wouldn't let Luca's strange behaviour ruin her trip; she would hold on to her fond memories of her time with Marco, Valeria and the girls and not let what had just happened spoil the last day and a half of her holiday.

***

As she queues at passport control at Heathrow Alice switches on her mobile and sees that she has a voice mail from Freya. There are about fifty people ahead of her so she decides to take the opportunity to call her friend. It turns out that Freya has had to come up to London for a meeting and is wondering if they can have dinner together tonight. Alice explains that she's just landed at Heathrow.

"Oh, forget it then darling. For some reason I thought you were coming home yesterday. It's just that I need to see a friendly face and have a natter. It's been a pig of a day and right now I'd rather slit my wrists than battle my way through rush hour crowds to get to Paddington."

Alice smiles at her friend's dramatic exaggerations. Life for Freya is never calm; drama is her oxygen.

"Don't be silly, I'm not going to turn down the opportunity of seeing you. I have to get on the Piccadilly line anyway, so I'll stay on until Piccadilly Circus and we can rendezvous in that brasserie you love."

"That's a great idea! I'll ring them straight away to book a table. D'you think you'll make it by 7 p.m.?"

"Yes, the queue's moving quite quickly now, so that should be fine."

"If you don't hear back from me in the next five minutes, you can assume I've booked. Can't wait to see you, darling, bye."

The journey into town is painless and, by the time she arrives at the restaurant, Freya is already there, sitting at the far side of the room. A huge wave of affection for her friend sweeps over Alice as she makes her way to their table. She's always guaranteed a good time with Freya because whatever is happening in their lives, they always end up laughing.

As Freya encloses her in a huge hug, she says, "Thanks for schlepping all the way into town; you're a star! Look, I've got us a couple of glasses of fizz." They clink glasses, happy to be together again.

"So, tell me, why has it been such a 'pig of a day'?"

"Oh it's been all about the implementation of some new bloody employment law and how we're supposed to deal with the new regulations. I've been bored to distraction all day, but I certainly don't intend to burden you with it all. So, how was Venice? Have you fallen out of love with the place yet?"

This was the only thing they have ever had a disagreement

about. Freya has never been able to understand "all this fuss about Venice". As far as she is concerned it's "just crumbling buildings, lots of water and too many people." It's a measure of the depth of their friendship that Alice is able to disregard her friend's views on the subject. If anyone else dared to voice a similar view in her company, Alice always took the opportunity to put them right.

"It was as magical as it always is, you philistine!" Alice replies in a mock stern tone. "You'll be glad to hear, however, that I actually left it for a whole day."

"Oh yes, you were going to visit those people you did translations for weren't you? How did it go?"

Before Alice can reply the waiter appears at their side, "Are you ready to order, ladies?"

"We'll both have the Prix Fixe menu and a bottle of your house red, please" Freya answers with a smile. There's a wide selection of dishes to choose from, but they always had the same thing: soup, followed by steak, which comes with a pepper sauce and a little tub of frites. After that, coffee and some petit fours.

With their order sorted out, Alice tells Freya all about her visit to the vineyard. As soon as she mentions Luca, Freya becomes very interested, firing a fusillade of questions at her.

"So, is he handsome? How old do you think he is? Is he attached? Did you fancy him?"

Alice sits back in her chair and looks at her friend. "Why do you still insist on getting so excited whenever I meet a new man? Haven't you given up on marrying me off yet?

"I live in hope darling, I live in hope. Go on then, tell me!"

"You're infuriating Freya, but I know I'll have no peace until I satisfy your curiosity, so, yes, he is handsome; I suppose he's probably in his late fifties and there doesn't seem to be anyone on the scene." Alice goes on to tell her friend about Luca's car, the vineyard, Marco's family and the *sagra*.

"And as for whether I fancy him or not, that's a tricky question. I did up until he shut down on me when we were chatting after the others had gone to bed last night. He'd been thoroughly charming the whole evening and then, whilst we were enjoying a nightcap, he asked if there is a Mr Thompson. I told him that there isn't, and assumed it would be OK to satisfy my own curiosity, so I asked him about Marco's mother and how come they hadn't got together. He was very reluctant to answer, so I didn't press it further.

This morning he seemed OK, and, as promised, he drove me around, giving me all the lowdown on the history of the area. But when we stopped for coffee, he had absolutely nothing to say to me. It all felt really awkward again, and then I remembered the photos - you know, the ones I developed from the camera I bought on my previous visit. I thought I could fill the silence by asking him if he recognised where they'd been taken. He looked at them for a few seconds then, suddenly, and without a word, he paid the bill, bundled me into the car and couldn't drop me off at the station fast enough!"

"How strange. Perhaps he was worried he'd given you the wrong idea the previous night by asking if you had a husband and then, after hearing about your ditzy idea of playing detective, he probably decided the safest thing to do would be to get away from you as quickly as possible!"

"I don't know what happened, but I have to confess that I do feel sad about it. I hadn't started fantasising that it was going to develop into some fairy tale romance – you've known me too long to realise that I'm not waiting for my prince to come - it's just that he's an interesting man whose company I had enjoyed."

"Mmmm, *just* a handsome Italian vineyard owner with a car to die for and who is, apparently, Italy's answer to John Travolta!" Freya laughs. "So, are you going to try to find out what made him behave like that?"

"Even though they were all so sweet - oh you'd love Valeria and Marco, they're a gorgeous young couple and have two adorable little girls - I have to remember that Luca's company is a client and behave accordingly. I'll send them a nice thank you card and see what happens. Come on, let's change the subject. Tell me how everything is in Bath."

"Oh Bath's fine. Bath continues to glide along at its own pace, and a very sedate one at that." Freya jokes.

"Oh, you mean us? Well, let me see. Georgie's first few weeks back at school as Head of English have gone well. She's already set up a debating club for the fifth and sixth forms and is happy that a decent number of kids have enrolled. There seem to be a few really talented speakers, so she's signed the school up to a debating competition. Each school takes a turn to host a debate and whoever wins the regional rounds goes forward to the final in London. The first debate is quite soon, I think. All very exciting.

She's also organised a creative writing club. She's had lots of girls turning up, but wants to get more boys to join. It's great to see her so fired up, Alice; I wish some of her enthusiasm would rub off on Rob."

"So, no improvement there?"

"No, not in terms of his state of mind, but, my God, he's looking quite dishy these days! He's lost about two and a half stones since he started his walking regime and he's finally agreed to let me take him shopping next week because all his clothes are hanging off him. You'll be pleasantly surprised when you see him next, I promise."

"Perhaps seeing himself in some trendy new clothes will give him a lift."

"The thought of anyone describing him as trendy would appal him as you well know Alice, but let's hope that seeing himself in some slim line shirts, new jeans and, perhaps, a new jacket, might raise his spirits. There are such gorgeous clothes for men around these days that I'm going to do my best to give him a transformation."

"I'll keep my fingers crossed and await a full debrief in due course! By the way, when does your train leave?"

"Nine thirty. Perhaps I'd better ask for the bill. At least getting a cab shouldn't be a problem should it? If you can't hail a cab in Piccadilly Circus, where can you?"

It takes less than a minute to find a cab and they arrive at the station with time to spare. As the driver sets off again, Alice is glad she accepted Freya's offer to stay on in the cab; it's such a treat, one she would never justify for herself. As much as she loves walking and sings the praises of public transport, this is wonderful.

***

Alice decides that she will post her thank you card the next morning and then, perhaps, she'll be able to close the door on the mixed emotions she's been experiencing since leaving Gorizia. She has such warm memories of Marco, his wife, the girls and the beautiful vineyard, but there's a deep ambivalence about Luca. At first, he'd seemed so at ease in her company, but his behaviour at the castle and the station had been unexpected and hurtful.

At a craft fair on Turnham Green a few months earlier she'd bought a box of cards featuring water colours of Chiswick by local artists. She digs them out from her desk drawer and decides to use one with a view of Strand-on-the-Green from the southern bank of the Thames. It features the 'Dutch' house with its blue and white shutters, basking beneath a watery winter sun, whilst the sleepy river rolls by in the foreground. She would love to own the original.

Dear Valeria, Luca, Marco, Antonella and Sofia,
Thank you so much for your hospitality. It was a pleasure to visit the vineyard and to be able to spend some time with you all. The sagra was so much fun too.
I'd like to take the opportunity to wish you continued success with the business and promise that I'll be flying the flag for Collio wines in future!
With best wishes,
Alice

She walks to the post box and drops the card inside. *'Che sera, sera'* she thinks to herself as she walks home.

***

Once her work is finished for the day, Alice decides to ring Georgie. The call goes straight to voicemail, so she leaves a message and goes outside to enjoy the late afternoon sunshine. Her little courtyard is looking pretty. The glossy evergreens and wispy ferns make it an oasis of calm. As she begins to sweep up some fallen leaves, her mobile starts to ring.

"Hi Georgie, thanks for ringing back. How are things?"

"Really rushed off my feet at the moment Alice, but it's all good stuff, so I'm not complaining. Are you back from Italy?"

"Yes, I got back last night and went straight from the airport to meet your mum who was up in London for a meeting. It was great to see her. She tells me you're doing lots of new things at school like setting up debating and creative writing clubs. Well done you!"

"Well, the previous Head of English had been in post for twenty five years. Can you believe that? Almost as long as I've been alive! I think he'd just run out of steam and had been coasting along to retirement for the past few years."

"In a way that's better for you though isn't it, because you can make your mark with lots of new ideas like the clubs you've set up. If he'd been brilliant and full of energy, he would be a hard act to follow."

"Yes, you're right. There are a lot of things I want to do differently, but I have to try to be patient. The trouble is that I've inherited my mother's impatience gene, so I'm finding it difficult" Georgie laughs.

At the senior staff meeting we had today the Head told us she wants to start a series of inspirational career talks for the fifth and sixth forms; she's new, too, by the way, and really impressive. She's asked each of us to come up with the name of someone who might be willing to come and give a thirty minute talk. We've got to submit a name, preferably with some relevance to our specialist area, by next Wednesday."

"Fantastic!" Alice blurts out almost before Georgie has finished speaking.

"What d'you mean?"

"Well, you're Head of English, and you're father's been in the publishing business all his life, so he'd be ideal wouldn't he? He could talk about careers in publishing and give advice to those who might have aspirations of becoming writers themselves one day. He'd be perfect!"

"Mmm. I should have thought of that. In my defence though, I have to say that I've only this minute come out of the meeting. The only problem is that with the way he is at the moment, I don't know if he'd agree..."

"Are you due to see him this weekend?"

"Yes, I promised I'd pop in to see them both tomorrow."

"Well, I would suggest that you tell him how much you want to impress the new Head. Ask him for his help. Tell him that it would be a feather in your cap if you could bring along a well known figure in the publishing world to speak at the school. I'm sure that, between you, you and your mother can persuade him."

"It's worth a try. Thanks Alice. Look, I'd love to chat for longer but there are a few things I need to sort out before the caretaker comes around jangling his keys. I'm sure mum will fill me in on all your news when I see her tomorrow and, hopefully, I'll be able to ring you with something positive to tell you about dad next week. Have a fun weekend. Lots of love, bye!"

***

What to do next? Suddenly remembering the long rogue shoots she'd noticed earlier on the star jasmine, she grabs her secateurs and, as she clips away, she starts to think about the photographs again. The challenge she's set herself is probably ridiculous, but she's determined to do her damnedest to at least find out something about the mystery woman if she can. And if she finds her, perhaps she'll find the camera's owner too.

She asks herself how a fictional detective would begin to solve the mystery? The first thing Miss Marple would probably do would be to speak to someone who might be able to tell her where the pictures had been taken. But that's what she'd tried to do when she'd shown them to Luca and it had been a spectacular failure. Who else could she approach? It would need to be someone who knew the area around Venice better than she did.

Maya! Alice feels sure that her ex student would be happy to help. She had tutored Maya for Italian GCSE and A levels and been impressed by the ease with which she had taken on the extra subject in both sets of exams. A natural linguist, Maya was now studying Fine Arts at Padua University.

Congratulating herself on her brain wave, Alice tears off her gardening gloves, grabs her phone and composes a text. She explains that she is trying to find out where some photographs were taken and asks if she can email a few scanned images to Maya in the hope that she might be able to help.

Less than ten minutes later the ping of her phone alerts her to Maya's response, which is that she'd be delighted to try to help. Alice scans a few of the pictures and emails them, along with a request that Maya should show them to her fellow students if she herself can't come up with anything.

She closes with:

And there's no hurry. Hope to see you when you're next in London. Love, Alice xx

***

Feeling pleased with herself, Alice decides it's time for lunch. Whilst she's standing in front of the open fridge trying to decide what she fancies, her mobile pings with another incoming message. It can't be Maya already, she thinks, but it is.

The test wasn't hard enough Alice!! Can you believe that the photos were taken in Padova? (Since coming here I can't bring myself to call it Padua anymore). The one with the bronze figure of a woman in it was taken across the street from Palazzo Moroni, the City Hall. I walk past her every day! Then, in one of the other photographs, your mystery woman is sitting on the edge of a canal with a open space behind her. Well, that's a park called Prato Della Valle and it's in Padova too.
What's the story behind the photographs? I have to say, the woman's very beautiful.
Happy to help with any further questions you might have.
Love
Maya x

Alice emails straight back with the story of how she comes to have the photographs and tells Maya about her mad idea of trying to get the photos and camera back to the original owner.

A few minutes later Maya responds:

That sounds like something that would happen in a film Alice! Wow!! Wait until I tell my friends about my super-cool, mystery solving Italian teacher!!!!!!M x
PS Maybe she was at the university, although she looks too old to be a student...

After reading Maya's email Alice sits staring at her mystery woman once again; she agrees with Maya and wonders if she is still so beautiful? Were the photographer and his model still together and, if so, where were they now?

***

A week after her return from Italy, Valeria phones.

"Hi Alice, how are you? I'm phoning to say thank you for your card. It was so good to have you here and to put a face to the name. Marco's telling all his business buddies to use you if they need anything translated, so you might get some new clients!"

"That's so sweet of him, Valeria; do thank him for me. How are the girls?"

"They're both fine, thanks. Antonella's at kindergarten and Sofia's having a nap, which is how I have the chance to speak to you.

Listen, Alice, do tell me to mind my own business if you want, but did something happen between you and Luca on the morning you left? Luca's been different since then, sort of super closed off."

"I'm sorry to hear that, Valeria. As you know, we had a night cap after you and Marco went to bed. At one stage Luca asked me if there was a Mr Thompson and I told him that there wasn't because I've never wanted to get married. Then, as he'd asked me a personal question, I felt I could do the same, so I asked him why he hadn't got together with Marco's mother. He was reluctant to answer, so I let it go, but the atmosphere between us had definitely changed somehow. We said goodnight and that was that.

The next morning he did what he'd promised and gave me a tour around Gorizia, but when we stopped for coffee at the castle, he had nothing to say to me and there was the most uncomfortable silence. I dug out some photographs and asked him to have a quick look at them as I'm trying to find out where they were taken. Luca scanned them very briefly and as he didn't actually make any comment about them, I assumed he didn't recognise anything. Then he suddenly announced that we had to go; I was deposited rather unceremoniously at the station and he drove off."

"How strange. He's has a good relationship with Marinella, Marco's mother, and he's always been happy to talk about her."

"Maybe he was just tired. Anyway, I'm sure you don't need to worry about him. He'll probably snap out of whatever it is soon, Valeria. "

"I hope you're right, Alice. I mustn't hold you up any longer."

"You're not holding me up; it's been lovely to speak to you. Don't forget, if you're in London any time, please do contact me!"

"I will, I promise. Oh, and I'd be fascinated to hear more about the pictures' back story if you ever solve the mystery!"

"Well, I do have a bit of new information. Apparently they were taken in Padova."

"Padova? Really? That's where Luca went to university."

"Oh.... Well..., maybe he pretended not to recognise them to save himself from being dragged into my silly little plan. I would probably have done the same thing in his place" Alice laughs. "Please don't mention any of this to him though; I'd hate him to think I've been talking to you about him behind his back."

"Of course, don't worry, I promise not to say anything. Bye

Alice. Have a nice day!"

She'd enjoyed chatting to Valeria, but now she had something new to think about. If Luca had studied in Padua, then why hadn't he admitted to recognising where the photographs had been taken?

She tries to put Luca's strange behaviour out of her mind and succeeds to a certain extent. What concerns her even more than Luca's brush off is why she seems to care about it so much. She can only describe her feelings as those of a teenage girl with a crush, which is nonsensical. In total, she's spent less than a whole day with the man for goodness sake, so why is she so affected by his behaviour?

She needs some distraction and wonders if she could ring Georgie. After checking the time and finding that it's already 4.30 p.m., she decides it's worth a try. Alice is curious to find out if the Head had OK'd her suggestion about Rob and, if so, to hear what his reaction had been. She's pleased when Georgie answers her phone.

"Hi, Georgie, Can you talk? I was just wondering how things are going at school and what's the latest on the talks?"

"Sorry, I did promise to let you know how things were going didn't I? Well, I went over for coffee the following day and started to tell dad about our new Head and how fantastic she was and how I really wanted to impress her. Then I explained about the talks and how great it would be if I could get a famous publisher like him to come and give a talk at the school. Instead of being flattered as I'd hoped, he was angry. He told was me that I was talking a lot of nonsense; he said that he'd never been a famous publisher and, anyway, he wasn't a publisher of any sort anymore. I did my best to persuade him, but he was adamant. There seemed to be no way I was going to be able to get him to agree to do it, so I gave up.

Mum had been sitting there listening to everything and not saying a word - I know you won't believe me, but it's true – but then, when dad got up to leave the table, she just exploded. She told him to stop feeling so sorry for himself and that it was time to snap out of it. She said that it wasn't as if he had anything better to do and if he couldn't do this one little thing for me, it was a 'poor bloody show'.

It was quite funny really; her outburst gave him a hell of a shock. Me too actually! We've all been pussyfooting around him for months and months now, waiting for him to sort himself out. I know how hard it's been for mum living with him. Eventually, he mumbled 'OK, if it's that important, I'll do it'. Mum punched the air, I gave him a big hug and that was that.

Dad ended up being the first speaker and came in to school last Friday. His talk was fantastic Alice. He soon had the kids eating out of the palm of his hand. Once he started speaking, he was transformed back into my 'old' dad; it was wonderful. The Head had sat in at the back of the hall and was very complimentary about his talk. She was almost flirting with him in the staff room afterwards!

I'm sorry I haven't phoned you, but I've been really busy. I knew this new job would involve more work, but I didn't quite realise how long all the paperwork and planning would take."

"Georgie, it's not a problem. I'm just so glad it was a success for you and for your Dad. So, how has he been since, although I suppose it's only been a couple of days...?"

"The talk was at the end of the day so I was able to go for a quick drink with him afterwards and he was almost bubbly. He admitted that he'd enjoyed it and the reaction he got from the kids - they'd had lots of questions for him. I think the Head's flattery did his ego a lot of good too. I also took the opportunity to tell him about the debating club I've set up. Our first competition is in October at a school just outside Bristol and he's offered to come along to give us some moral support. It's brilliant, Alice!

Since then, he's been telling mum that he might offer to give the kids some tips on public speaking if I'd like him to. She's so relieved to see him genuinely interested in something at last. I'm not going to overwhelm him, but I would love it if he could do something similar for the kids in my creative writing club. After all, he's an expert on what makes for good writing. Of course, all this would need the Head's approval and he'd have to go through a police check, but I'm hopeful."

"That all sounds marvellous, Georgie. I'm so pleased. And what else is new?"

Georgie laughs, "Nothing else really Alice. I'm so knackered at weekends that all I want to do is sleep and catch up with school work. There don't seem enough hours in the day at the moment."

"Well, remember all work and no play ..."

"Yes, I know. I'm sure things will get easier; it's early days. I do have a wedding to look forward to though at the end of next month, which will be fun."

"Oh, lovely; is it one of your Bristol friends?"

"Yes, it's Julia. It sounds as if it's going to be amazing. Her fiancé is Scottish and they're getting married in a lovely old hotel, right on the edge of a loch. It'll be a late afternoon wedding so it should be really romantic, with lots of candles and flaming torches. I can't wait."

"I'll want to hear every detail about the wedding when I

next see you. It's time I came down again, so I'll speak to your mum and ask her to liaise with you about possible dates."

"Perfect. I'll WhatsApp you some photos from the wedding. Must go, thanks for calling, Alice. Big hug, bye."

***

The weeks fly by because of the quantity of work Alice has to deal with. She's always busy in September as Italian businesses get back to normal after their August break. Things usually calm down again around the last week in October and she welcomes this little hiatus in her work schedule as it allows her to do things at home that she's let slip. After that, there will be the usual rush to clear projects before the Christmas holidays.

This quieter period means that she can also do some sleuthing as far as the photos are concerned; she knows she'll always regret it if she doesn't explore every possible avenue open to her. What exactly does she know? Well, she knows that the shop owner bought the camera at a Railway Lost Property Sale in July 1982. She doesn't know where the sale took place, but feels that she can assume that it was in Venice or somewhere in the Veneto region. When she'd lost her laptop three years ago on a train in Rome and gone to inquire if it had been found (it hadn't been) she'd been told that if property wasn't collected within six months, it was sold off. That must be the same throughout Italy, surely? So, if that was the case, the camera was most probably lost at some time between January and June 1982.

Next, she needs to think about the protagonists in her little mystery. Were they visiting Padua? Was anything special happening in Padua in the first six months of 1982 that had caused them to go there? She doesn't know much about Padua, other than it has the second oldest university in Italy. What other attractions could have drawn tourists there in 1982? Back then, there weren't cheap flights into small regional airports which would have made visiting lesser known European cities easy. Perhaps there'd been some big trade fair or international art exhibition? After an hour on-line when she's discovered nothing of any significance, she remembers that they could, of course, be locals. Not knowing what to do next and feeling totally deflated, she decides to give up for the day. Thank goodness she's going out tonight.

***

It had been Paul's birthday a few days ago and she's arranged to take him to dinner. They'd met about ten years ago through mutual friends; he was newly divorced, so Alice had been drafted in *just* to keep the man/woman ratio correct, her friend had told her. She understood that her friend's motives came from the right place, but she always hated these set-ups. Married couples appear to be unnerved by the unattached. Is it that they want their single friends to be blessed with the same 'blissful state of matrimony' they themselves 'enjoy', or are they secretly afraid that the unattached might actually be having more fun than them? Probably a mixture of both, she had decided at the time.

In this particular case, however, she did have to thank her friends. Paul had turned out to be the perfect dinner companion. He worked in the city for a bank and, when they met, had recently found himself a house in Barnes. He hadn't tried to impress her; he was quietly funny and interested in what she did. They soon started seeing each other regularly. Both of them enjoyed walking, the cinema and theatre and gradually their friendship deepened. Sex with him was uncomplicated and funny, in the best possible way. Laughter was a defining characteristic of their relationship and everything had been perfect for a couple of years.

That was until the evening Paul proposed. They'd just got back to her place after a trip to the cinema to see the latest Indiana Jones film. Alice had never been a Harrison Ford fan, but she couldn't refuse to go to see it as Paul had recently sat through *Mamma Mia* with her the last time they'd had a film night.

Alice hadn't seen it coming. Her reaction when she heard the words "Alice, will you marry me?" was a feeling of total panic. All she could think was "Oh no, why is he doing this? Why is he spoiling everything?" Thank goodness he hadn't bought a ring - he'd planned to take her to The Lanes in Brighton the following weekend to choose one. It had all been terrible. She'd tried to make him understand that she did love him, but that marriage just wasn't for her. She had felt terrible for hurting him. He hadn't shouted, or left, slamming the door behind him, perhaps it would have been easier if he had. Instead, he said he understood, wished her well and left.

In the following weeks she'd spent a lot of time worrying about Paul. Could she, should she, ring him? She knew she wasn't going to change her mind about getting married, so it had seemed best to do nothing. She was ashamed to admit that she was also concerned about what her friends would think of her. Would they decide she was heartless? She needn't have worried because Paul had never told them what had happened.

The girlfriend who'd introduced them had once asked why they weren't seeing each other anymore and the only response Alice had been able to come up with was "Oh, we had a silly disagreement."

Then, in mid December she'd received a Christmas card from him. Seeing his handwriting on the envelope had given her such a thrill. The message inside read:

> *How about a Christmas drink with an old friend?*
> *Love, Paul*

Alice's eyes had filled with tears. She did want to see him again and he had written 'old friend...' Before she could over think things too much, she'd phoned him. They arranged to meet in their favourite pub a couple of days later and their relationship was rekindled. They saw each other often, took short holidays together and were happy. The "M" word was never mentioned and it was tacitly agreed that they could see other people if they wanted to. For Alice it was the perfect arrangement and she hoped that Paul felt the same way too.

***

Alice is looking forward to seeing him and wants to make a special effort with her appearance tonight. In the end, she decides on a simple sage green velvet dress which she knows Paul likes and a pair of suede kitten heels in the same shade of green. She's decided to treat herself to a taxi as it's quite a walk to the restaurant. The food and the service are excellent and the staff don't rush you so that they can reuse the table, which now seems to be the habit of so many popular London restaurants.

Paul is already there when she arrives. He stands and gives her a hug.

"I know tonight's your treat, but I've ordered us some drinks. I took a chance on a Campari Soda for you; is that OK?"

"Just what I fancy, thank you."

Alice sits and takes a long, appraising look at Paul. She has to admit he's looking particularly handsome tonight. He's wearing a suit she hasn't seen before; dark navy, with a fitted jacket and slim lapels. His almost blindingly white shirt is teamed with a slim navy tie.

"My, you're looking rather gorgeous this evening!"

"Thank you ma'am" he laughs. "You look as elegant as always."

Alice smiles, "I think we make a handsome couple, don't we?"

Paul doesn't respond; instead, he begins to study the menu with great concentration. After a moment, he looks up and says "Shall we decide what we're having before we catch up on our news?"

As they eat, Alice fills Paul in on Georgie's new job and the fact that, with any luck, Rob might be on the mend. Paul has always got on well with Rob and is pleased to hear that things are improving for him. They go on to chat about what's been happening in the lives of their mutual friends. Satisfyingly replete, they fall into a companionable silence which she uses as an opportunity to check out their fellow diners.

Paul waits until Alice, her curiosity satisfied, makes eye contact with him once again and then, with a strangely awkward smile, drops his bombshell. He starts by reminding her of the deaths of two of his oldest friends in the last ten months and explains how these events have caused him to re-evaluate his life.

"To cut a long story short, Alice, I've recently finished negotiating an early retirement package so that I can finally do all the things I've never been able to do in the past, either because I didn't have the money, or the time.

You know how much I love sailing, don't you? Well, I've decided I'm going to buy myself a boat."

Alice can't believe what she's hearing. Early retirement? Buying a boat? She's never shared his passion for sailing. Out of a sense of duty, she'd once agreed to join him for a cross channel jaunt in a boat he sometimes crewed for and had hated every second. All those trips down to Southampton recently now begin to make sense to her...

She realises that Paul is waiting for her to say something. She smiles and says "That's brilliant, Paul. Goodness me, what a piece of news! I need a moment to process it all... If it's how you feel, of course you should go for it. I assume you'll be able to manage financially?"

"Oh yes. I started paying into a pension at twenty one, so money shouldn't be a problem."

She is in a state of shock and doesn't know what to say next.

"I have something else to tell you, Alice."

She can't imagine what else he can have to tell her and begins to feel uneasy. "I think I might need a drink before you share any more momentous news with me, Paul." She catches the waiter's eye and orders a grappa.

"Would you like something else?"

"A whisky please."

They wait slightly awkwardly for their drinks. Fortunately,

the restaurant has begun to empty, so their order arrives quickly. Alice knocks back her shot of grappa, takes a deep breath, smiles and says, "OK, go for it, I'm ready."

After what seems like an age, Paul looks directly at her and says:

"I've met someone, Alice."

She can't believe what she's hearing. Somehow she manages to force her lips upwards into a smile of sorts and says, "Tell me all about her."

It seems that he met Pamela at the yacht club in Southampton about ten months ago. They know the same people and have crewed a few times on the same boats. She's a widow and passionate about sailing, too.

Alice sits there feeling numb as Paul excitedly lists the rest of his plans for a new life. Once he's left the bank, he's going to move into Pamela's house in Lymington and, as soon as the money comes through from the sale of his house, he'll finalise the purchase of the boat. After that, he and Pamela plan to sail away into the sunset for a year. He looks so incredibly happy as he tells her about everything and, because she loves too much to want to dim his joy, she does her best to convince him that she's delighted for him.

"It sounds as if you've met the perfect woman at the perfect time, darling. I'm really happy for you. Perhaps I'll get the chance to meet her some time." She takes Paul's hand and squeezes it in an attempt to reassure him that she means what she is saying.

They collect their coats and get into the taxi the waiter has called for them. Alice looks across at Paul and puts her arm through his. He smiles back at her, "Are you OK? I know it must all have come as a shock."

"It was certainly a shock, but I'm fine. I'm truly happy for you, I promise."

They're back outside Alice's house in minutes. Thankfully, she manages to hold herself together just long enough to give Paul cheery wave before slamming her front door shut behind her and bursting into tears.

***

The next morning she gets up at five thirty, tired of tossing and turning. It had been a long night. She'd lain in bed feeling desperately sad and sorry for herself, which was ridiculous. After all, she'd been the one to set the ground rules of their relationship and Paul had gone along with them, even though he'd always made it clear that he'd wanted more. It had been she who had airily once said that she wanted them to feel free to see other people if he wanted to.

What was that old saying? 'Be careful what you wish for.' She hadn't wished for this, that's for sure. How could she not have sensed that their relationship had changed, that he was seeing someone else? She had genuinely believed that Paul was happy with their arrangement because, after the hiccup over his proposal, he'd never brought the subject up again. And now he's met someone else. Someone with the same love of sailing, who is happy to be a part of his dream. She doesn't begrudge either of them their happiness, but she suddenly feels so exposed and vulnerable without Paul as the backstop in her life.

As always, when she experiences a major set-back, she needs to talk things through with Freya. They've always been there for each other. Alice picks up her mobile and begins to type:

Have a sudden desire to see you all. Would there be any chance I could come down tomorrow and stay a couple of days? I quite understand if it's inconvenient so DON'T HESITATE TO SAY NO.
Love, Alice xxx

Freya replies immediately.

Would love to see you. Is everything OK? Sorry, can't ring to chat because I've got back-to-back meetings today. I don't know if you'd fancy it but Georgie's school's first debating competition is taking place near Bristol tomorrow night. Rob's offered to go along, so how about you catch a train to get you into Bristol for, say, 5 p.m. Rob could pick you up and then you can get a bite to eat together before the competition starts at 7 p.m. After that, stay as long as you want. Love F xxx

Alice texts straight back with an enthusiastic 'thank you' and begins to feel a little better.

***

She catches a train from Paddington station which will get her into Bristol at 4.45 p.m. Happy at finding a table seat, she catches up on some work whilst the train whizzes westwards. They arrive on time and, as she walks along the platform, she enjoys that sense of excitement she always experiences at railway stations or airports. She loves seeing the smiling faces of people meeting up and empathises with those who look sad as they wave someone off.

She realises that she hasn't been back to Temple Meads

since she left university in 1980! Of course, she's passed through it many times en route to Bath, but is happy to see it again. There are new shops and signage, but the fabric of the station is still the same, with its fifteen platforms and huge curved roof. Alice wonders what her twenty one year old self would think of the woman she is today?

She makes her way out of the station and positions herself where she can see the cars driving into the drop off area and only has to wait about five minutes before she spots Rob's car. After flinging her suitcase in the back, she jumps into the passenger seat.

"Hi. Thanks for picking me up."

"No problem."

He swings the car confidently around a couple of parked cars and joins the main road. "I've been thinking that our best bet is to get out of Bristol and stop at a pub I know that's only about five miles from the school. It's not a fancy gastro pub or anything, but it serves acceptable pub grub. Does that sound good to you?"

"Yes, that suits me fine. I didn't have any lunch, so a plate of sausage and mash or fish and chips would fit the bill perfectly!"

Rob hasn't quite been transformed back to his old self yet, but he does seem to be more relaxed than when she last saw him. She forces herself not to ask any questions about how he's feeling and what he's been doing. Hopefully, he might open up to her whilst they eat.

The pub turns out to be a genuinely old inn, with dark wooden beams supporting a low whitewashed ceiling. They decide on a table next to the open fire before Rob goes off to get the menu and the glass of lager which Alice suddenly fancies. After some thought, they decide on sausage and mash for Alice, and lamb shank for Rob.

Once she's finished her first mouthful of smooth mash and rich gravy, she turns to Rob. "I'm looking forward to listening to the debate. We used to have a debating club at my school, but I was never brave enough to put myself forward. The thought of getting up and speaking in front of a crowd of people still fills me with terror. What about you?"

"I don't remember if we had one, to be honest. The only extracurricular activities I was interested in involved a rugby ball or cricket bat!" Rob laughs. "I was never shy though and once I started working, I quite enjoyed giving presentations.

By the way, I don't know if the girls mentioned it, but Georgie asked me to go and give a talk about careers in publishing at her school a while back."

Alice pretends to think about it for a moment before replying, "I think she might have mentioned it in passing. How did it go?"

"To be honest, I was unhappy about being emotionally blackmailed into doing it by them both, but once I got there, I really enjoyed it. With all you hear on the news about schools these days, I quite expected to have to face a noisy, unruly mob, but I was pleasantly surprised. A lot of them were genuinely interested and surprisingly articulate. Some of the pupils I spoke to afterwards mentioned they were in the debating club as well, so I thought I'd come along tonight to give them and Georgie, of course, some moral support."

"That's sweet of you Rob, I'm sure they'll all be pleased to have you there."

They finish their meal and return to the car. Rob finds the school without needing to resort to his car's SatNav. 'Can't stand the bloody things, maps never let you down' has always been his mantra. They make their way to the hall and spot Georgie and her three debaters standing near one of the two tables which face out over the body of the hall. Most of the front row of seats are taken by people whom Alice assumes are friends and family of the teams; three seats remain empty and have 'Reserved' signs on them. Alice decides that they must be for the adjudicators.

She and Rob grab a couple of seats in the second row as the hall starts to fill up. Georgie pops over to them, "Thanks for coming" she whispers, "I keep telling the team to relax and enjoy the experience, but my stomach's churning!"

At seven o'clock the Head of the school sweeps into the Hall and welcomes everyone to what he says he is sure will be an interesting and thought provoking evening. The topic for debate is 'Single sex schools are better for all students".

Georgie's team are proposing the motion and are very convincing, with well thought out arguments. The first boy and the girl speak confidently, but it's their last debater, a boy who must be about seventeen, who is particularly impressive. He's perfectly at ease and is even able to bring an element of humour into his argument, which is enjoyed by the audience. The other team give an adequate performance, but both Alice and Rob feel certain that Georgie's team are clear winners. The adjudicators leave the hall and the noise level and sense of anticipation rises as everyone waits for the result. After ten minutes the Head leads the adjudicators back into the room. The room quietens as the chief adjudicator stands to give a well balanced critique of both teams. Then, he pauses, a tad theatrically, before announcing that Georgie's team has won and will now go through to the next round. Both teams shake hands and everyone claps politely.

Once Georgie has an opportunity to congratulate her team and speak to their parents, she comes over to Alice and Rob. "Wasn't that incredible?" she says as she hugs them both. "I'm so proud of them. Thank you for coming. One of the parents gave me a lift here and needs to leave now, so I can't chat. I'll ring you tomorrow, Alice. Give my love to mum and thanks, Dad, I can't tell you how much your being here tonight has meant to me."

Rob's quite fired up by the whole experience. "They were very good considering it was their first time weren't they, Alice? Of course, if they're going to win the competition they'll need more practice and some tips on projecting their voices, how to stand, all those little things which make an audience relax and enjoy your argument."

"Well, I'm sure they'd be grateful for any tips you can give them if you can spare the time Rob."

"Mmm, perhaps I'll have a word with Georgie."

***

When they get back, Freya is eager to hear how it all went and is thrilled to be told that Georgie's team had won. The three of them agree to have a cup of tea together before heading off to bed.

"Sorry, I have to go in to work tomorrow, Alice, but we'll have the weekend to catch up. I'm assuming you can stay at least until Sunday afternoon?"

"If you can bear to have me, I'd love to stay until then."

"Are you sure you're OK, Alice. Has something happened?"

"I'm fine and all the better for being here with you."

Freya doesn't seem convinced, but she lets it go.

***

Next morning, after hearing Rob get up and take the dogs out for their morning walk, she creeps downstairs to make herself a cup of tea before Freya surfaces. She scribbles a note to her friend saying that she will cook dinner tonight for the three of them, then retreats back to her room. She's washed and dressed by the time Rob gets back and wonders whether the dogs enjoy these long morning walks as much as Rob appears to. He seems quite bright and tells her that once he's finished his tea, he's off to help a friend assemble a new greenhouse.

"It'll take most of the day. Will you be OK here all on your own?"

"Of course I will! Actually, there's a bit of research I want to do. After that, I'll walk down to the village and get a few things for dinner. I'm going to cook by the way."

"Thanks Alice, I'm looking forward to it already! Right, well I hope you have a productive time with your research. See you later."

Whilst she'd been showering that morning, Alice had decided she would have another go at searching for anything which might help with the mystery of the photographs. Perhaps this a subconscious diversionary tactic to keep her mind off Paul and his new lady?

She scours the internet, looking at the myriad sites which appear when she types the words "Padua early 1980s". The list seems endless, but she ploughs her way through them. Most of the sites cover the city's history, whilst others gave information on its industry and population. A little frustrated, she decides to refine the search to 'News Padua 1982' and this time she discovers a great many links to a kidnapping. Italy was a very dangerous place to be if you were rich or important in the 1970s and 1980s because kidnappings were frequent.

She begins to read the first article which scrutinizes the history and activities of the Brigate Rosse, or Red Brigades, an anti-fascism far-left group. Apparently, they'd been formed in the 1970s with the aim of destabilisation and the eventual establishment of a revolutionary state; their plan was to achieve this through bombings, robberies, kidnapping and murder. Alice suddenly remembers that five members of the then Italian Prime Minister's security team had been killed when he'd been captured by the Brigate Rosse; Aldo Moro himself had been kept hidden for fifty four days before being assassinated. The murder had rocked Italy and been big news around the world.

She discovers that in December 1981 four Red Brigade members, posing as plumbers, had entered the flat of Brigadier General James Lee Dozier, the US NATO Deputy Chief of Staff who was stationed in Verona. They'd tied up his wife and daughter and kidnapped the general. Dozier was the first foreigner to be kidnapped by the BR, who held him for forty two days in a flat in Padua. A team of specialists from the Italian police had eventually rescued the general and, at the same time, had captured a BR member who'd been left in the apartment to guard the hostage. His instructions had been to kill Dozier if the police should arrive, but, thankfully, he wasn't able to carry out his instructions.

The more she reads, the more appalled she is by the havoc

the BR had caused in Italy between 1969 and the mid 1980s. At their height, apparently, they had four to five hundred active members and up to a thousand followers who helped them periodically. It must have been a terrible time to live through; one article informs her that those years were called the *Anni di Piombo*, The Years of Lead. None of her Italian friends had ever discussed the subject with her, but she understands that it must be a period most people would prefer to forget.

***

Alice loses all track of time and is shocked to realise how many hours she has been at the computer. It's time to do something about dinner, so she pulls on her coat and sets off down the lane which leads to the centre of the village. Three different people speak to her en route, which leaves her slightly unnerved. This rarely, if ever, happens in London, where the rule is to avoid making eye contact at all costs.

The village still has a pub, a sub post office inside the community shop and a butcher's, owned by a local farmer. No problem with the provenance of the meat here. She spies some pig cheeks in one of the trays and decides that she'll use them to make a casserole. Cooked long and slow they are delicious. She also picks up some King Edward potatoes to make a bowl of buttery mash (she'd enjoyed the mash at the pub so much), a Savoy cabbage and some carrots. As for a pudding, she was undecided. She liked baking, but using someone else's oven is always tricky. In the end, she picks up a tub of vanilla ice cream which she'll scoop into three of Freya's pretty glasses and then 'drown' with warm espresso to make *affogati*. It's the easiest of desserts, and tastes spectacular.

Alice enjoys preparing the meal and once the casserole is in the oven, she takes herself off to her bedroom, where she lies down, trying to second guess the plot of the book she'd started last night.

Freya is the first to arrive home and shouts 'hello' as she opens the front door. Alice hears her throwing her keys down onto the hall table as the dogs rush to greet her with some excited barking. Alice waits at the top of the stairs until the dogs are satisfied that their 'mum' is happy to see them too and then asks, "Good day? Bet you're dying for a drink. Go and sit down and I'll sort it out; tea, coffee or a glass of wine?"

"A glass of red, please. I've got that TGIF feeling. It's almost worth going to work just to experience the joy of Friday evenings!"

"I agree" Alice replies as she carries in two glasses of red wine, "Friday nights are special, aren't they? Even though I don't work in an office, I still feel the thrill of the end of the working week."

Freya accepts the glass gratefully. "So, come on, open up about why you needed to see us so urgently. Don't look so defensive - you know we love to see you, but, tell me, what's happened?"

"I just wanted to see you all, isn't that allowed...?

Freya doesn't answer the question. Instead she raises both eyebrows and stares back at Alice.

"OK, you're right; I did have an ulterior motive for coming down. I met Paul the other night because I'd promised to take him to that restaurant he loves on Devonshire Road as a belated birthday celebration. After we'd finished our meal, he suddenly blurted out that he's decided to take early retirement!

I don't know if I told you, but he's lost a couple of old friends in the last year and it's made him reappraise his life. Apparently, he wants to satisfy a long-held dream of owning a boat and going on some long voyages, so he's selling his house to fund his dream."

"Bloody hell. Well done that man! It's a brave thing to do isn't it? So where's he going keep this new boat? He's not intending to live on it surely?"

"No, he's not. There was more news."

"Oh my God, he hasn't asked you to marry him again, has he?"

"No, just the opposite; it turns out he's met somebody. A woman called Pamela who lives down in Lymington. She loves sailing and he's moving in with her." Alice's voice is beginning to tremble.

"Come over here so I can give you a hug. Oh, darling that must have been a terrible shock for you. What did you say?"

"Oh, you'd have been proud of me, Freya; I congratulated him and said I was happy for them both. I even managed to say that I'd love to meet Pamela some time! But when I got home, I couldn't stop crying. I should have known this would happen. After all, Paul never made a secret of the fact that he wanted more from me, but I just assumed he was happy with our arrangement. Deep down, I do want him to be happy. If giving up his job, buying a boat and moving in with this woman will make him happy, I do genuinely wish him all the best. It's just that I'm shocked by how abandoned I feel. You know I've never wanted marriage or to live with someone permanently - I tried it once with Peter, and that didn't end well did it? So why has this hit me so hard?"

"I'd completely forgotten about Peter..." replies Freya,

shaking her head.

"I suppose I deserve it. If I'm honest with myself, I realise I have been a bit smug about managing to live my life largely on my terms."

"Oh, I don't know about that; over the years, quite a few of my friends would have jumped at swapping places with you."

Alice leans forward and picks up her glass, "I know I'll be fine once I get used to it all..."

Would she be OK though? Lovely, reliable, considerate Paul, always there when she needed him. But no longer. At that moment, her father's exasperated voice fills her ears, "Well my girl, you've made your bed, and now you have to lie in it!" If he were here now, he would tell her to stop feeling sorry for herself and offer what was his panacea for any problem, a strong cup of tea.

"Thanks for letting me come down, Freya, I really appreciate it. Please don't ever tell me that you're planning to bugger off somewhere as well, will you?"

They hear the back door open.

"No darling, I won't. Come on, let's go and see what sort of a day Rob's had. What's cooking by the way, it smells delicious."

Dinner is a success, with Freya and Rob happy converts to the delights of pig cheeks. They reminisce about old times and old friends and it's exactly what Alice needs. Rob hasn't asked why she suddenly decided to visit; he's always made it clear she is welcome here.

The greenhouse building had gone well and, of course, he and Phil had just had to go to the local pub to celebrate. Rob mentions that when he was there, a couple of 'the boys' were talking about going to a point-to-point in North Devon tomorrow. Would Alice and Freya be interested? Determined to try to get Alice to agree, Freya pipes up with "They're actually quite fun and there's also shopping to be done if you're in the mood. Lots of interesting stalls."

"Oh, well, in that case" laughs Alice, "count me in."

After a hearty breakfast prepared by Rob, they set off and have a wonderful day. It's possible to bet on each of the races, which adds extra excitement to the whole thing. Alice manages to come away with an elegant pair of water-proof brown suede and leather boots. Sadly, Georgie is busy for the whole weekend so Alice doesn't get to see her, but they do manage to speak on the phone and agree that Georgie will come up for a weekend sometime before Christmas.

***

As she catches the London train, Alice realises how much better she feels than when she'd travelled down only a few days earlier. She's looking forward to tackling the three translations she has lined up for the coming week and is feeling more positive. After settling herself into her seat, she checks her tablet and is pleased to find an email from Maya.

Hi Alice,

Hope you're well. I wanted to let you know that I haven't given up on trying to help you with the mystery lady in those photographs. When you first contacted me I did tell all my friends about you finding the camera and the photographs and they all wanted to see the pictures you sent me because they thought it was such a great idea.

As you know, nothing came of that, but I was at a party recently and a group of us were sitting around after most people had left, when one of the girls asked if I'd managed to find out any more information about your lady. Her boyfriend was interested to hear what we were talking about, so I told him the whole story. He suggested that I put up a few flyers with a photograph on some of the notice boards in the university.

At first, I was a bit doubtful about doing that, but his argument was that perhaps some of the staff who have been around for years might recognise her. Anyway, I printed out some A5 sheets with one of the photos - the one where she's laughing - asking anyone who might know her to contact me. Nothing happened until yesterday.

I got a call from someone who's been an administrator at the university for years and years and she thinks that your mystery woman could have been a lecturer here in the late 1970s and early 1980s. She wasn't sure, but she thought she might have worked in the Political Sciences Department.

As you can imagine, I was really excited and so this morning I went to the university library to find out if there were any publications which included photographs of lecturers for the period we're interested in. They sent me down to the archives and, with the help of one of the staff down there, I found her in an old prospectus! CAN YOU BELIEVE THAT???? Her name is Silvana Rossi and she did work here as a lecturer. The prospectus was for 1980.

I felt like the heroine in a Dan Brown book!!! Don't groan, Alice, I know you think his books are rubbish, but for a few moments I was the attractive young heroine digging out a vital piece of information in an international mystery!!

I'll try to find out more, but I've got two big essays to research and write, so we'll both have to be patient. It should be easier now that

we have a name though, shouldn't it? I promise that as soon as I
find out anything else, I'll be straight in touch.
Hope to see you when I'm back for Christmas!!
Love, Maya xx

Alice can't quite believe that Maya has managed to find the woman; she's tingling with excitement. Now, at least they know her name, Silvana Rossi, and, somehow, that makes her so much more 'real'. Poor Silvana, she'd waited, unclaimed, in the photographer's shop for so long.

Alice retrieves one of the images she'd emailed to Maya and sits, looking at it.

"Ciao, Silvana Rossi, I'm so glad I know your name at last."

Will they be able to find out any more about her? She's sure that Maya will have already done an on-line search for the name, but can't help tapping the name into the search engine. A long list of Silvana Rossis appears, but none of them is 'her' Silvana.

She keeps being drawn back to Silvana's face and wonders again what sort of a woman she was, or, hopefully, still is? There are so many questions Alice wants to ask her. Were you in love when these pictures were taken? Where are you now? Are you happy? As she questions Silvana, she begins to question herself too. Is she herself happy?

She considers how to answer, but realises that she doesn't honestly know. If she'd been asked the question before her last trip to Venice, she would have replied without hesitation: "I have a career I enjoy, a home I love, an 'honorary family' whom I adore and a close relationship with a man I respect. So, yes, of course I'm happy."

But her world has changed. First of all, she's met Luca and, despite her best efforts, thoughts of him have continually buzzed around inside her head since her return to London. Each day, the realisation of how much she had enjoyed his company has grown stronger; she has sometimes even allowed herself to consider the ridiculous possibility that she could have been the woman to free him from whatever sadness he seems to keep bottled up inside himself. Of course, it helped that he was handsome and charming and interesting and also happened to have an Alfa Romeo Spider! But whenever these thoughts have crossed her mind, she has forced herself to remember the way he behaved towards her on the day she'd left Gorizia. It had all been going so well. What had happened?

And then, of course, there was Paul. His news had upset her more than she cared to admit because she'd assumed, foolishly as it turned out, that their 'perfect' arrangement would last forever. Now, she felt certain that she'd be receiving a wedding invitation within the year. Deep down, could that be what she wanted for herself someday? All the certainties in her life were suddenly being challenged.

***

At *Tenuta Grauner,* Marco is sitting in his office. He should be feeling extremely happy. The weather this year had been kind, with no late season hail storms to devastate their crop as sometimes happened. They'd had a bumper harvest and it looked as if it was going to be an excellent vintage. He stares out of the window towards the cascading lines of vines surrounding the farm house. His thoughts are interrupted by a pair of hands sliding over his shoulders as Valeria kisses the top of his head.

"What are you thinking about?"

"Nothing much."

"Come on, I know you too well. Why don't you take a coffee break? We've got thirty minutes before I go to collect the girls."

Marco smiles at his wife and follows her into the kitchen. He watches as she unscrews the aluminium stove top coffee-maker every Italian household owns. She carefully fills the coffee reservoir and pours fresh cold water into the base of the machine. The whole procedure is like a well choreographed ballet. It never ceases to amaze him that this beautiful creature left her family, thousands of miles away, to come and live here with him and his father. She's made him so incredibly happy and, not content with that, has also given him their two beautiful daughters. Thanks to her, his dream of having a 'normal' family has become a reality.

"So come on, out with it, I know something's been eating away at you."

"You're right, as always. It's *papá*. Nothing new; you've heard it all before. I just wish I could find out why he is the way he is. The sadness or regret, or whatever it is that keeps the very core of him closed off from me, I don't know why it's so important to me, Valeria, but it is. And it seems to have got worse recently.

I know I should be grateful for what I've got. He's been a good father who's shown me nothing but love and support. OK, I would have preferred him to have married my mother, but I've accepted that. I want to understand why he's never found anyone he's wanted to share his life with. What stops him? Every time he meets a new woman and starts seeing her, I hope that she will be the one who will wipe out whatever it is that always makes him pull back, so that, finally, he will become his real self. But it never happens.

It's silly, but I had this wild romantic idea that perhaps he'd fall for Alice. He seemed to enjoy her company and seeing him laughing and dancing with her at the *sagra* made my heart soar. But nothing happened after she left and now he seems to be even more closed off than ever before. I can't imagine that she would have done anything to upset him....."

"Did you ask him about it at the time?"

"Well, I didn't ask him outright if Alice had upset him" Marco shrugged, "but I did ask if everything was OK and he said it was."

"Oh God, men! Why are they so afraid of opening up?"

"That's unfair. You know I'm not like that. But *papá* is different; he never discusses his feelings with me!"

"You're right, I'm sorry. I can fill you in a bit about what happened with Alice if you like. I haven't mentioned it before in case you'd feel uncomfortable about my talking to her."

"Well, it's done now, so you might as well tell me what you've managed to find out."

"OK, let me pour the coffee. A few moments later, Valeria brings two small black and red espresso cups to the table and sits down opposite her husband.

"I really liked Alice, Marco. She was great company and so easy talk to and, like you, I was convinced your father was quite taken with her. It would have been sad to let the connection I'd made with her fizzle out, so, when she sent us that pretty thank you card, I gave her a ring to thank her for the thank you card! Don't roll your eyes!

I told her I was glad to hear that she'd enjoyed her visit and we chatted for a while about how you were getting on, about the girls and the *sagra*. I noticed that she hadn't mentioned Luca at all and, because of how distant Luca has been recently, I decided to ask her if anything had happened on her last morning. She was reluctant to say anything initially, but then she did admit that Luca did behave a bit strangely. She wondered if it was because of something she'd said back here after the *sagra*. It turns out they'd chatted after we went to bed and Luca had asked her if there was a man in her life."

"What? *Papá* asked such a personal question? I can't believe it; it's his life credo never to ask personal questions."

"Well, he did and she told him that there wasn't anyone. Then, because he'd asked her about her love life, she'd felt it would be OK to ask him why he hadn't got together with your mom. Apparently he seemed very uncomfortable with her question, so she didn't press the matter and they said goodnight. Next morning he took her on the little sightseeing tour he'd promised, but when they stopped for coffee he had nothing to say to her and there was a long uncomfortable silence.

She was desperate to find something they could talk about, so asked him to look at some photographs because she was interested in finding out where they had been taken. She thought that Luca might be able to help. Apparently he wasn't at all happy about being asked to look at some random photos and had barely looked at them before he stood up and announced that they had to leave immediately. He rushed her to the station, and just roared off."

"I can't understand why he would behave like that...."

"He has been distracted and distant since then hasn't he?"

"Yes, he has," Marco nodded sadly.

"I know you've asked your mom in the past if she knows

why he is the way he is and she hasn't been able to come up with a reason. What about your uncle Roberto? Might he have an answer?"

"I don't know. Roberto left to go to university in Turin when *papá* was nine and he made his life there. I doubt he'll be able to tell me much. "

"Surely it's worth a try though Marco? I know you'd be so much happier if you could find out something about your father's life before you were born which might explain the way he is. Go on, you've got nothing to lose, have you?"

"Let me think about it."

"No, do it now. I'll look forward to hearing what Roberto has to say when I get back from picking up the girls."

Marco has no idea how he is going to broach the subject with his uncle and he feels guilty that he, too, is now going to be discussing his father without his permission. But, Valeria is right; he does want to be able to understand his father better.

His uncle retired a couple of years ago so Marco knows it's OK to ring him during the day. He dials the number.

"Pronto, Roberto Grauner."

"*Ciao zio* , it's Marco. Are you free to talk?"

"Ah, *ciao* Marco. Yes, I'm in the car. It's good to hear from you. How is everyone? Well I hope?"

"Yes, thank you, we're all fine." For a moment Marco doesn't know where to begin.

"This is all going to sound very strange, but I have a question about *papá*. It's about the way he is. Has he always been so, I don't know how to put it, so 'cut off' emotionally? In the past I've tried to convince myself that it's just the way he is, but, there must be a reason surely? I suppose having my daughters has made me think about family relationships more deeply recently. Don't get me wrong, he adores the girls and Valeria. And you know how much I love him *zio*, it's just that I would like to understand him better. Why has he never married or, at least found someone to share his life with? I've always felt that there's some sort of regret, a sadness, deep inside him."

Roberto sighs in response. "*Oddio*, Marco, such deep questions! Let me think. I suppose he was different when he was growing up. Obviously, we weren't close because of the age gap between us, but I do remember him as a happy, outgoing little boy. He was very close to your grandmother, I know that. He used to confide all his secrets to her and she was proud of that, let me tell you!

I remember coming home one summer and being asked if I had a girlfriend. When I wouldn't satisfy her curiosity, she said 'Why can't you be more like Luca, he tells me everything!' I remember replying, Mamma, he's ten years old so, of course, he tells you his little secrets. Wait another ten years and then we'll see how much you know about his life!"

"And were you proved right?"

"Yes and no. I seem to remember that when he was in his first couple of years at Padova, he'd still tell her about his friends and whenever Mamma asked if any of the girls in his group were 'special', he'd reply that they were 'only friends'. Of course, she had her own methods of trying to find out more information. She'd arrange to meet up with Pietro's mother - he was in the same year at Padova - and they'd share any news they'd managed to find out about what their boys were up to. In the end, he did start to tell her a bit about his girlfriends, but, from what I remember, *mamma* never had to worry too much, because none of them ever developed into anything serious.

Wait a moment, now I come to think of it, there was a change in his behaviour when he was in his last year at university. He didn't come back to visit your grandparents as often as he had previously, but he was always happy and upbeat when he spoke to your grandmother on the phone. She continued her usual methods of surveillance via Pietro's mother, but I don't think she discovered anything particularly interesting."

Marco wished he'd spoken to his uncle years ago. His father never talked about his time in university or what he had got up to. Whenever he'd tried to find out if his father had ever done anything wild as a student, the answer was always the same, "Marco, I was an extremely boring student I promise you. No skeletons; I just kept my head down with my books. Sorry to disappoint you."

"So he never told you anything about his love life either?

"No. Afraid not. We didn't see each other very often because I was working in Turin by then. When we did speak, our conversations were usually about the important things in life, Marco, like football and what sort of vintage it would be that year."

"And you can't tell me anything else that might have happened to him?"

"I don't think so. Hang on a minute, there *was* a big drama just after Luca had taken his finals. He'd always promised our parents that he'd join the family business as soon as he completed his studies, but on the day after his last exam he phoned to announce that he'd accepted an offer of a job in a vineyard near Bordeaux. Apparently, they wanted him to start straight away, so he wasn't going to come home. His justification was that he wanted to have experience of how other vineyards operated before starting work back there. He said he knew he could improve the management of the business, but now he also wanted to see what actual improvements and new techniques he could bring to the production side.

Of course, our parents were upset. Well, that's a bit of an understatement; your grandfather was furious. Your grandmother just wanted him back home. Luca eventually sent her his new address, so she was able keep in touch with him by letter. Gradually, things calmed down and your grandfather accepted that, perhaps, it was not such a disaster for Luca to get some experience of how they did things in France. A year later he came back."

"And how was he when he got home?"

"He was totally focussed on the changes he wanted to make, of course! You know how stubborn my father was, well, Luca inherited his stubbornness from him, so your poor grandmother didn't have an easy time of it in those early years. It's strange how I'd forgotten about all this Marco. I do now remember *mamma* telling me once that he had changed when he got back from France."

"It all sounds terribly strange to me, *zio*. First, he stops coming home on visits and then, without warning, he takes off for France. What could have happened to cause it all? There must be more to it."

"I don't know Marco; I wish I could help you more."

"Don't worry, I'm grateful for what you've told me. If you remember anything else, of course, I'd be grateful to hear about it. Please give my love to the family. Are you coming to us for Christmas as usual?"

"I think your aunt and Valeria have already arranged all

that. Yes, we'll be there. Give my best to Luca, Valeria and the girls."

Marco mulls over what his uncle has told him. He isn't that much further forward, but his uncle had, at least, fleshed out *papá's* back story a bit. As soon as Valeria gets back he'll pass on what he's learned to her, sure that, by the end of the day, she will have come up with at least three possible scenarios to explain what might have happened to *papá*. What fascinated and intrigued him at this precise moment though, was how history had repeated itself. He and Luca had both initially disappointed their fathers by deciding to go abroad to work at other vineyards.

***

Marco isn't the only person who has been thinking about the past. As Luca makes his way back down the hillside after an afternoon repairing a gate on the northern edge of the property, the thoughts, which he has been trying to block out all day, break through and begin to swirl around inside his head. In the months since Alice's visit, Luca has found it increasingly difficult to control the emotions which he's managed to bury for so many years. It's still difficult for him to look back on what happened with any sense of calm analysis. All those years ago, he'd been too young, passionate and stubborn to see anything other than his own viewpoint. How he regretted running away to France.

But it's not just that. There's also the effect Alice had had on him. He is still surprised by the strong connection he had felt to her from the moment they shook hands. She was attractive, funny and independent, all qualities he prizes in a woman. And there had been a moment, as they were dancing, when he'd imagined, for just a nanosecond, what it might be like if she were to become a part of his life. He remembers the shock it had been to realise how much the idea thrilled him.

If only she hadn't questioned him about Marinella. To have answered honestly would have involved telling her everything, but he couldn't do it. Fortunately, she'd been intelligent and sensitive enough not to force him to explain, so things could still have progressed. If only she hadn't asked him to look at those damn photographs. What must she think of him?

Exhausted by the emotions overwhelming him and needing a drink, he makes for the kitchen where he finds Marco and Valeria deep in conversation. So intent are they on whatever it is they're discussing, that they don't hear him enter.

"That looks like a very serious conversation you're both having!"Luca calls out.

Startled by the sound of his voice, they turn towards him. For an instant they both look guilty, but manage to recover their composure fairly quickly.

Marco smiles at his father."*O ciao papá*, we didn't hear you come in!"

"Obviously. I have to say you looked like two teenagers up to no good."

Valeria gets up and, walking towards Luca, jokes, "Gee, now wouldn't that be fun? To be young and carefree again and doing something naughty?"

Luca is curious to know what their conversation had been about, but it's none of his business. After all, he's the last person who has the right to demand to know the secrets of others.

***

Back in London Alice is happily preparing dinner. Georgie has kept her promise to visit London and should be here at any moment. Alice usually organises interesting things for them to do together, but this time Georgie has suggested that they wait to see what they both fancy doing when she arrives.

Once she's finished in the kitchen, Alice gives the house a quick once over, anxious that everything is perfect for Georgie's arrival. She has decorated a small Christmas tree with baubles collected over many years and placed a large vase of greenery from the garden on the table near the front door.

Georgie arrives rosy-cheeked, sporting a pretty white pom-pom topped woollen hat.

"Gosh, the house looks pretty!"

"Thank you. Now, would you like a drink and a chat first, or would you prefer to eat straight away?"

"Can we eat? I'm starving. I had to arrange an extra rehearsal this lunch time, so didn't have a chance to grab anything."

"Of course, come and sit at the table. I've made a huge lasagne. I thought I could divide up the leftovers so that you can take some back with you on Sunday. There's a tub of your favourite ice cream for later if you fancy it."

"That all sounds perfect, Alice, and it would be even more perfect if I could pour myself a glass of wine!"

"Go ahead and pour us both a glass while I dish up. So, how are rehearsals for the production going?"

"Well, they were going reasonably well, that is until yesterday, when everybody seemed to have forgotten everything they've learned. Hence the rehearsal this lunch time. I have to admit they were much better today, probably because I let them know exactly how pissed-off I felt after their abysmal performance yesterday! The thing is, everyone's tired by this stage in the term, teachers and pupils. I'm sure they'll be fine on the night."

"How many performances?"

"One in front of the whole school and two evening performances for family and friends. We should get a good turnout. *Bugsy Malone's* always popular. This is delicious by the way; can I have seconds when I finish?"

"You don't need to ask; I'm glad you're enjoying it. And how are mum and dad?"

"Mum's fine. Busy at work as always, but really pleased that Dad's slowly reverting to his old self. Your idea of getting him to give the career talk was brilliant. Since the debate you both came to, he's got even more involved by giving the kids advice on how to be more effective debaters. They really like him and he's come along to all the competitions. Sadly, we got knocked out in the semi-finals last week, but it was an impressive result for first timers and we've recruited quite a few new members. I'm sure we'll do equally as well, if not better, next year.

Dad's also supporting the creative writing club I started. We've got almost as many boys as girls coming to the sessions, which is brilliant. Dad's presence has a great deal to do with that. Interestingly, the Head always seems to have time to pop in to see how things are going, which I find very amusing! She's even trying to persuade him to become a governor."

"And is he still doing the long distance walking?"

"Yes, but not in that manic way he was. He's much more relaxed about it all now.

And what about you, Alice? Mum told me about Paul. How are you feeling about it all now? Have you met the new woman yet?"

"Oh, I'm fine Georgie. I was sad for a while, but we all have to accept the consequences of the choices we make, don't we? No, I haven't met her. Actually, I'm glad he hasn't tried to set up a meeting because I'm not quite ready for that yet.

Have you thought about what you'd like to do tomorrow?"

"Well, what I really fancy is a trip to Portobello; it's ages since I was last there. My girl friends and I have decided on token presents from now on and we've set a limit of £10. I'm sure I'll be able to find some interesting bits and pieces there. I haven't got anything for mum and dad yet, either."

"That suits me fine; it's been a long time for me, too. The only thing is, it does get very busy, so you'll need to get up early. We can grab some breakfast when we get there and then go in search of some bargains before the hoards arrive."

**

Having both slept well, they're excited to set off next morning. They take the tube to Notting Hill, arriving at 8.15 a.m. Most of the antique dealers scouring the stalls at the Notting Hill end of Portobello Road have come and gone by now, so they have no difficulty in finding a seat in a pretty little cafe, where they order pots of tea and two English Breakfast rolls. When the waitress brings their order, they can't help laughing. The rolls are enormous, each one crammed with sliced sausages, rashers of bacon and a fried egg. They tuck in after agreeing that this gargantuan breakfast is fully justified because they have lots of walking and shopping ahead of them.

Portobello is exciting whatever the time of year, but, with Christmas approaching, it has a special magic; stall holders sport Father Christmas hats, fairy lights are everywhere and there's a general air of excitement. By the time they've finished their rolls and emptied their pots of tea, they are ready for some serious shopping.

Alice suggests they visit a new place nestled between the antique and book shops on the hill leading down from Notting Hill first. It sells traditional British men's clothes, shoes and accessories, all with a slightly modern twist. Georgie loves everything they have on display and picks out an olive-green waxed canvas and leather backpack for Rob.

"This will be perfect for Dad when he comes to school. At the moment he uses his old business briefcase which looks all wrong. This isn't bulky or overly trendy. What do you think, Alice?"

"I think he'll love it. It'll work well with the new clothes he's had to buy since he's lost all that weight."

Georgie also finds a narrow, dark sage-green knitted tie with tiny navy spots. "I think I might get him this, too."

"Very nice. I can guarantee he'll like it because he had a tie exactly like that when I first met him with your mum. I haven't quite decided what to buy him, but it'll probably be a large bottle of that spiced rum he loves."

They continue to walk down the hill until they reach the section with stalls selling fruit and vegetables. The pyramids of different coloured fruits look amazing, the red pomegranates setting off the orange satsumas and mandarins perfectly. Piles of glossy chestnuts fill the spaces between apples, pears and pineapples. Next comes Alice's favourite flower stall, which she always stops to admire as the array of flowers is guaranteed to be breathtaking. She promises herself that she will return later to pick up a couple of bunches of scarlet gladioli.

By crisscrossing the road they are able to make sure that

they don't miss any of the stalls. In the tented area under the Westway they find a fabulous multi-coloured resin chain necklace and both agree it's the sort of statement piece Freya will adore. Nearby, there's a stall selling 'vintage' head squares which Georgie immediately decides will make the perfect gifts for her friends. Alice decides to leave her searching through the vast pile whilst she goes to get them a couple of coffees. Her phone rings as she is standing in line. A quick glance at the screen tells her it's an Italian number.

"*Pronto.*"

Alice can't hear a thing because, at that moment, the Salvation Army band decides to start playing "Once in Royal David's City".

She presses her fingers over her other ear and shouts, "I'm sorry, I can't hear you, the music's too loud. Hang on a moment, while I find a quieter place." There's a residential street a few yards away so she makes for that. "OK, go ahead. I should be able to hear you now."

"Hi again Alice, it's Valeria. I hope you're well. Gee, where are you? It all sounds very Christmassy, wherever it is!"

"I'm in Portobello with my goddaughter and, yes, it does feel wonderfully festive here. How are you all?"

"We're fine, thank you. The girls are getting very excited about Christmas. Look, I won't hold you up and I probably shouldn't be calling you at all, but I wanted to let you know that Luca is flying to London today; he's just left for the airport. Marco had set up a meeting with the buyer for a chain of Italian restaurants in London tomorrow, but he's come down with the most awful cold, so he can't make it and Luca's decided to step in. Look, Alice, I might be barking up completely the wrong tree and he probably has no intention of contacting you, but I've come into the office to check on something and your website's details are on the screen. Have I done the wrong thing phoning you? Marco is always telling me off for poking my nose in where it doesn't belong."

Alice's heart is beginning to race, but she forces herself to keep her voice calm."Don't give it a second thought, Valeria. It's lovely to hear your voice. Poor Marco, please give him my best wishes and tell him that I hope he feels better soon. And as far as a visit from Luca is concerned, I'm pretty certain that he has absolutely no desire to see me again. There's probably some simple explanation; perhaps one of the other vineyards have asked him for my details? Anyway, please don't worry. Give Antonella and Sofia a kiss from me. I hope you all have a wonderful Christmas."

"Thanks, Alice. *Notting Hill* is my all time favourite movie, I wish I was there with you. Bye now, Merry Christmas!"

Alice remains rooted to the spot as she considers how she feels about the news that Luca will soon be in London. In the end, she comes to the conclusion that she is excited and nervous in equal measure. And whilst she does believe what she said to Valeria about Luca not wanting to see her, what if he did turn up? Immediately irritated by her foolishness, she orders herself to put such a silly idea out of her mind and to concentrate on getting the coffees. Fortunately, the queue has dispersed, so she's soon back with Georgie.

"Oh, thanks, Alice, I need a shot of caffeine. What do you think of these?"

In her absence, Georgie has found what she thinks is the perfect headsquare for each of her friends.

"I'll wash and iron them and then wrap them in some pretty tissue and ribbons. I think the girls will love them."

They remind Alice of the beautiful scarf she'd worn in Luca's car. No, she mustn't let herself think about him.

"They're perfect Georgie."

They spend a few minutes savouring their coffees and, although the smells coming from the food stalls opposite are very tempting, they're still full from their huge breakfast rolls. There are a lot more people around now, although there's still room to move around reasonably comfortably.

Alice suggests that they walk up to the intersection with Golborne Road, where the stalls continue. Georgie soon spots a late 1930s/early 1940s wall plaque of a woman's face. Pointing it out to Alice, she whispers, "Isn't that gorgeous? Mum loves this type of thing."

Alice agrees that Freya would definitely like it and looks unsuccessfully for a price tag.

"I love it, Georgie, but these plaques go for anything up to £200 pounds if they're kosher and in good nick - I know, because I've always fancied one for myself."

The stall holder smiles. "You're right, my lovely; originals can go for even more than that, but that one's a good quality reproduction and it's forty quid."

The plaque personifies the spirit and fun of the 1930s perfectly. It's a profile of a bob-haired brunette with a pretty retroussé nose, cupid bow pouting lips and fine dark eyebrows. She's wearing an orange cloche hat with a thick band of green around the brim and her slender neck curves elegantly down into an upturned white collar.

"She's beautiful, even if she is a reproduction. I'm going to get her, Alice."

Their energy levels are now starting to flag, so they decide that it's time to make for home. Rather than try to fight their way through the tide of people streaming down from Notting Hill, they use side streets to get them to where they can catch the bus back to Chiswick High Road.

As a number 94 approaches, Georgie asks Alice if she's happy to go upstairs. She always loved riding around on the top deck as a child. Despite the bus driver's violent swerve back into the stream of traffic, they manage to make it upstairs safely and are both thrilled to see that the front seat is empty.

"This is fun!" they agree as they take in the crowds on both sides of the road, laden with Christmas purchases. Only now do they realise how exhausted they are. The bus crawls westward from Notting Hill and, after changing buses, they make it back to Alice's house after what seems like an eternity. They kick off their shoes, Alice makes a pot of tea and they both slump down onto the sofa.

"It's been a good day, Georgie and you've managed to find some great presents."

"Yes, it was fun wasn't it? I've got an idea Alice. Rather than you cook for me again tonight, why don't I treat you to supper at the Bull's Head?"

"There's no need, I'm happy to knock something up for supper you know, but, if that's what you'd like to do, I'm very pleased to accept."

"Good. Look, I'm zonked, I think I'll go up and have a little nap before we go back out."

"Go ahead, I might even stretch out here and have forty winks myself."

They both benefit from their naps and enjoy their trip to the pub. The food is tasty and they spend the evening chatting about everything under the sun. Alice is so grateful for the easy and close friendship she has with her goddaughter. She would love to know if Georgie has heard anything about Mike, but decides it's best not to spoil their evening by mentioning his name.

***

The next morning Alice decides to let Georgie sleep in. When she does finally surface after eleven, she pads downstairs in her pyjamas and oversized bed socks. The poached eggs on toast Alice prepares for her soon disappear, and then she is shooed back upstairs to shower and pack her bag because Alice has ordered a cab to make sure she gets to the station in plenty of time for her train.

All too soon, the taxi's outside. Just like her mother, Georgie flies down the stairs in a whirlwind. As Alice stands in the doorway waving to her, Georgie winds down her window, blows a kiss and shouts "See you in two weeks at mum and dad's!"

Closing the door behind her, Alice is overcome by a sense of sadness. She goes upstairs to check that Georgie hasn't left anything behind. It still smells of Georgie's perfume, which makes Alice sadder still. What is she going to do with herself now? There are no translations waiting to be done, her paperwork is up to date, the house is quiet and she's alone.

She wanders aimlessly back downstairs. Here she is, exactly where she's always wanted to be, the mistress of her own life. But her precious independence doesn't seem to be making her very happy at this precise moment, does it...?

Previous experience has taught her that an effective antidote to a bout of self-pity is a brisk walk, so that's what she'll do. She pulls on a thick pair of socks and her 'point-to-point boots', zips up her old parka and grabs her gloves. It will be dark in a couple of hours, but there's still time for a decent walk. To stop herself wallowing in self pity, she decides to plug in her ear phones and catch up on the Archers' omnibus she missed this morning.

By the time she reaches Kew Bridge she's engrossed in Shula's problems at the stables and in the Grundy's latest money-making scheme. Her spirits rise as she strides out over the bridge, glad to be walking, rather than a prisoner in one of the cars crawling along at a snail's pace. When she gets to the other side, she turns right and takes the steps down onto the tow path. Despite the cold wind, there are quite a few boat crews skimming along the surface of the Thames. She overtakes various family groups and a couple of dog walkers and begins to feel better. After a while, she turns left, out onto Kew Green and slows her pace as she walks past the large and imposing houses which face the green.

Windows blaze with lights so she's able to check out the Christmas trees and decorations inside. Some front doors are guarded by bay trees adorned with small, twinkling lights, whilst others sport expensive wreaths. Seeing them reminds Alice that she's forgotten to put up her own wreath and resolves that it will be the first thing she does when she gets back. After a circuit of the Green, she re-crosses the bridge and makes for home.

As soon as she arrives she goes straight to the shed and unhooks the wreath from the back of the door. She painted it pale grey last year and it still looks OK. Back in the kitchen, she dampens an old cloth and gives the willow ring a quick clean. Once the cobwebs and dust have been sent packing, she retrieves the trio of silver bells her mother used to use on her Christmas wreaths and secures them firmly in place. Next, a plush red velvet ribbon is tied into a bow at the top; now, all she has to do is to attach the wreath to the front door. When she realises that she's still wearing the thick pair of old socks she'd had on inside her walking boots, she can't resist the opportunity to take a little run out of the kitchen and launch herself forward across the parquet in a delicious long slide towards the front door. Her pre-walk mawkishness has vanished. As she slows to a halt, through the glass panels of the front door she notices the silhouette of someone making their way up the path. The security light clicks on. It's Luca.

She opens the door.

"*Buonasera,* Alice."

She stands there, the wreath still hanging off her left arm, and waits for him to speak. He looks different to the man who'd said goodbye to her at the station. He seems nervous.

All she can think of to say is, "I was just about to hang this on my front door..."

"Can I help?"

"Yes you can, actually. I normally have to go through the palaver of dragging a kitchen chair out here to fix this into position. There's a drawing pin in the middle of the top edge of the door. I usually wind the twine at the back of the wreath around the drawing pin and when I'm happy that it looks OK, I tie a knot and snip off the excess and then drag the kitchen chair back of course..."She's gabbling.

She watches quietly as he follows her instructions. Satisfied, he looks up and gives her a questioning smile.

"It looks lovely; thank you for your help Luca. Would you like to come inside?"

She's amused when she realises that she was speaking to him in English. Does she, perhaps, subconsciously need the protection of her mother tongue to deal with whatever Luca has to say to her? She reminds herself that she mustn't let him know that Valeria has phoned her.

"So, Luca, how come you're in London? Is there something you need my help with?"

"No, no, Alice this is...", he pauses, searching for the right word and then giving up. "*Una cortesia*".

"A courtesy?"

"Exactly, a courtesy!" He's definitely looking extremely uncomfortable.

Alice forces herself not to fill the silence. It had been her downfall the last time they'd been together.

"I am so sorry for the way I behaved Alice; it was extremely discourteous. Will you please accept my sincere apology?"

Alice looks steadily into his eyes and, after a moment, responds.

"Thank you, Luca, I do accept your apology, but I must tell you that I have gone over what happened so many times, trying to work out what on earth I did to upset you. You did dump me rather unceremoniously at the station, you know."

Luca slumps back into the sofa, "Yes, I know I behaved badly and that's why I am here. I have come to explain. But it's a long story and I think I might need a glass of something to give me courage."

"I have some Irish whiskey if you'd like some?"

"Thank you."

She makes her way into the kitchen where she keeps her bottles of booze and, ducking behind the partial wall dividing it from the sitting room, pulls off her baggy socks and checks her hair in the glass door of the oven. Not brilliant, but acceptable, is her verdict. She places a glass of red wine, the bottle of whiskey and a squat tumbler onto a tray before walking back through into the sitting room where she sets it down on the coffee table in front of Luca. He carefully pours himself a whiskey, but seems to be either unable or unwilling, to continue with his explanation. The silence and air of tension between them becomes uncomfortable and Alice can stand it no longer. Before she can stop herself, she says,

"Luca, I've made some progress with the pictures I showed you in Gorizia; would you like to hear what I've found out?"

Why is she bringing the photographs up again? He'd stormed off the last time she showed them to him!

As he doesn't respond, she decides to plough on.

"To be honest, Luca, the disdain and lack of interest you showed in the photographs made me even more determined to keep trying. Once I'd looked into that woman's eyes, I became quite obsessed with her. Eventually, I hit upon the idea of contacting an old student of mine who's studying at Padova University in the hope she might be able to help - she knows the Veneto region really well. To cut a long story short, she recognised that the location was Padova. Maya actually walks down the street where some of the photos were taken every day. And, you won't believe this, but after some research in the university archives, she managed to find out the woman's name. She's called Silvana Rossi. It turns out that Silvana was a lecturer in the Political Sciences Department at the university in the early 1980s."

She waits for some reaction from Luca once again. Would he now explain why he had chosen not to tell her that the pictures had been taken in a city he must know so well? He sits there saying nothing and a wave of annoyance starts to wash over her. Finally, he meets her eyes.

"First, I have to admit that I lied to you by omission, Alice. When you showed me the photographs, I knew immediately where they were taken and I also recognised Silvana."

This time it's Alice who is shocked into silence.

"This is why I have come to you. To explain everything. I took a business studies degree at Padova University. I had no interest at all in politics, but I had a friend from Trieste who was always telling me about one of the professors on his course. He kept on and on, 'Marco, you must come to listen to her. She's amazing. Very beautiful, and very passionate. She's a Marxist and we are all ready to man the barricades with her after her lectures!'

I have to admit that I was intrigued, so I went along one afternoon. My friend was right, Silvana was the most beautiful woman I'd ever seen. No make-up, jewellery or expensive clothes, she was a pure force of nature. I fell in love with her at first sight. I know people never believe that it can happen - I was one of them until I saw her - but I knew in that moment that no other woman would ever do for me."

"I admit I didn't actually listen to anything she was saying; all I wanted to do was to sit there and look at her. After the lecture my friend told me that some of the students were going, as usual, to a nearby bar and that Silvana, sometimes, joined them. Of course, I jumped at the chance of possibly getting to speak to her, or even just spending some time in her company.

I was lucky and about an hour after we got to the bar, she appeared at our table. She greeted everyone by name and when she got to me, she raised her eyebrows and asked 'And who is this?' My friend explained that I was from Gorizia and was also studying at the university. She looked at me and asked me 'which department?' When I told her business studies, she shouted theatrically 'Beware a capitalist lackey!' and pulled the trigger of the imaginary gun she was holding to my forehead.

Everyone roared with laughter, of course, but then she smiled and said, 'Perhaps, we should try to convert him rather than shoot him' and, pulling up a chair next to me, said, 'I might as well get started now!'

I was subjected to the full force of her argument for the rest of the evening. Gradually, the others left to go to home or meet up with friends until, finally, only the two of us were left. Silvana didn't seem to care about eating or drinking; all she cared about was 'the fight'. I asked what had made her so passionate about politics and her answer was, 'My mother's milk. Both my parents were partisans in the war. They vowed to fight capitalism and fascism and were prepared to die for the cause if necessary. I feel the same.'

I was overwhelmed by the force of her beliefs, but I'd never been a political person. Neither had my parents. They'd seen too many horrific things happen to their friends because of politics. It had all started in the early 1930s with knocks on the door in the middle of the night for anyone who refused to join the Fascist Party. Then, after the fall of Mussolini, came the reprisals from the partisans against the fascists or those households which refused to put the partisans' *bandiera rossa,* the red flag in their windows. Both sides doled out the same punishments. Enemies were taken up into the mountains to be shot and their bodies hurled into one of the many deep caves or ravines of the *Carso*. Somehow, my family managed to keep their heads down and survive. I didn't tell Silvana all this, of course.

At about eleven, the bar owner told us he was closing up. Silvana was amused when I asked her if I could walk her home.

'Oh my God, a gentleman! I suppose I can't stop you walking alongside me if that's what you want' was her answer.

When we got back to her flat, she told me I was 'a sweet boy' and invited me to go up. She was so different from the girls I'd been out with. Of course, she was different; she was a professor and twelve years older than me! I was totally overwhelmed by her. In the morning, she was gone. It was a shock to wake up and find myself there and remember what had happened the previous night. I pulled on my jeans and sweater and walked around the flat. It was pleasant enough. Clean and ordered. No pretty feminine touches anywhere, only hundreds of books stacked in neat piles.

I couldn't resist looking in her wardrobe for some reason. It was a huge old mahogany thing and was only about a third full. Her clothes were functional, with no bright colours, and I remember thinking that she didn't need fancy outfits - she could wear a sack and still look beautiful. I left the apartment and, as I closed the door, I wondered if I'd ever be invited back."

Luca pauses and, finishing the glass of whiskey, points to the bottle "May I?"

Alice nods. After a few minutes, he restarts his story.

"I didn't know what to do next. Should I try to 'accidentally' bump into her at the university, or attend another of her lectures? I couldn't decide. What I was certain about was that I shouldn't tell anyone about how the evening had ended. When I next saw my friend, he wanted to know what I thought of Silvana and what had happened when the rest of them had left. I just told him I'd got another lecture on the need to overthrow the government and establish a revolutionary state.

I didn't want anyone to suspect what had happened, so I

kept away from the Political Sciences department for the first few days, but, in the end, I couldn't bear not seeing her, so went and hung around the main entrance to the Political Sciences Faculty. When she finally emerged carrying an armful of books, I called out '*Professoressa*, can I help you with those?' She laughed when she saw me and said, 'Why not? I was wondering when I'd you see again.'

We went back to her flat and made love. That's how it was; she never wanted anything more from me. She never asked me anything about my private life and, apart from the time she told me about her parents, she didn't give me any personal details, ever. At first, that was OK with me. I was a red-blooded young Italian who was having great sex with an intelligent and experienced older woman; who wouldn't be happy with that? My finals were coming up and I had to buckle down if I wanted to pass. So, with that excuse, I didn't meet up with my friends and what little spare time I did have, I spent at Silvana's flat. She was happy with the arrangement. Not that she was always available though; she was often involved in things she never saw fit to tell me about, and I didn't question her.

We'd been seeing each other for a few months when I had the idea of asking her if she would spend a whole day with me after my final exams were over. I had set my heart on a romantic trip to Venice. I longed to be able to walk around with her openly. Although I'm sure she never gave a damn about what people thought of her, she had told me that she was in trouble with the university authorities because of her political views and was determined not to hand them something which they could use against her, like having a relationship with a student. Of course, friendships between male lecturers and female students were accepted as normal! But, in the end, she gave in and agreed to my plan.

On the day after my last exam we arranged to meet at the railway station at seven. I wanted to have as much time in Venice with her as possible, but when I got there, I found her in the middle of a large group of striking railway workers. She explained that her 'comrades' were holding a twenty four hour strike. As you can imagine, I was furious that our romantic day together wasn't going to happen. Silvana, of course, would have been happy to stand shoulder-to-shoulder with the strikers for the rest of the day, but, in the end, I managed to drag her away.

I remember her teasing me, 'You're like a little boy who's been told he can't have an ice cream. Cheer up!' When she caught sight of the camera I'd slung around my neck, she raised her eyebrows and asked, 'A Leica, is it yours?' I explained that it was a gift from my family and asked if she would let me take some pictures of her.

'Well, I suppose you're no longer officially a student of the university now, so OK, but only a few because I loathe having my picture taken.'

Despite what she'd said about hating being photographed, she didn't stop me from finishing the whole roll - well you know that already don't you?"

"Luca, you look exhausted; would you like to pause and perhaps have something to eat? I've had my goddaughter here for the weekend; she left straight after lunch, so I don't have much to offer you other than some bread and cheese. I could make you some Welsh Rarebit. Have you ever tried it? It's one of our British 'delicacies'!" Did he recognise the irony in her voice? And what on earth is she thinking, interrupting his retelling of an important love affair to offer him *a slice of Welsh Rarebit!?!*

He's obviously decided to humour her because he nods and follows her into the kitchen where he watches as she starts to make a roux with flour and butter. She's secretly amused by the look of horror on his face when she adds beer and cheese to the mixture; the horror deepens when Worcester sauce and English mustard join the mix.

"Could you cut me two thick slices from the loaf for me, please? You'll find a bread knife in the drawer in the table. Then put them into the toaster, please." As soon as the slices of toast pop up, Alice loads them with a generous amount of the cheesy mixture and slides them under the grill.

"Just stand there and keep an eye on them while I set the table. Shout out as soon as the cheese starts to brown and I'll whip them out. Would you like to finish off the bottle of beer?"

"Yes, why not?"

A few minutes later Luca announces that the cheese is browning.

"I'm sorry, but I don't even have a lettuce leaf to serve with this! I must be fulfilling every negative preconception foreigners have about the British and their terrible food."

Determined to pretend to enjoy it, Luca picks up his knife and fork, "No, not at all, I'm looking forward to finding out what this tastes like!"

Alice smiles back at him. He's not so bad really, she decides.

"And why is it called Welsh Rarebit? What does it mean?"

"I don't know Luca. I think it used to be called Welsh rabbit and somehow, along the way, the name got changed. So, what do you think? Go on, be honest, I promise not to be offended. Anyway, it's your fault for turning up unexpectedly."

Although she is grateful to be discussing something frivolous, Alice begins to worry that Luca won't continue with his story.

"I'm surprised, but I have to admit that it's delicious, Alice. I was quite worried when I saw what went into it, but I'm happy to be proved wrong!"

It doesn't take them long to finish their meagre slices of toast. "I'll just pop the dishes into the dishwasher; why don't you make yourself comfortable back on the sofa? Would you like a coffee?"

Luca nods and makes his way back towards the sofa, stopping en route to look at the photographs on one of the side tables. "Is this your family?"

"As good as. They're my oldest friends: Freya and Rob, whom I met at university and their daughter, Georgie, who you just missed. Sadly, just like me, my parents had no brothers or sisters, so when they died I felt terribly alone, but Freya and Rob took me under their wings and supported me through it all. I love them to bits, but they live in Bath, so I don't get to see them as often as I'd like to. I'll be with them for Christmas though, which is always wonderful."

"I'm glad you have them Alice. They're obviously very good people."

"They are Luca, they really are. I'm so grateful to have them in my life, but I'm also lucky to have good friends in London to call on when I feel like company. I'm also happy with my own company though, it's one of the few pluses of being an only child." Alice hates to think anyone might feel sorry for her. She hands Luca his coffee and they sit in silence for a few minutes. Then he starts to speak,

"It's taken me a long time to admit that I've handled things very badly; I should have told my family the whole story years ago. Only now have I been able to admit to myself how I've allowed what happened to affect my life and, more importantly, Marco's.

When I'd used up the roll of film, Silvana suggested that we go back to her place. To be honest, I was disappointed. I was tired of our furtive meetings in her flat and had imagined that our special day would end with dinner in a romantic restaurant. As soon as we got back I turned the radio on, hoping that some music would raise my spirits. All I could find on any station were news reports. There'd been a bombing in Milan. No-one seemed to have any definite information on how many had been killed or injured, but what was known was that the Red Brigade had claimed responsibility.

I suppose my frustrations and disappointment about the day and my horror at how these evil people were prepared to further their cause loosened my tongue and I said that they were all animals and beneath contempt. Silvana wasn't prepared to let my comments go unchallenged and started dragging out all the usual dogma I'd heard so many times before. In the past I'd been prepared to let it all wash over me because I loved her so much, but that day, I couldn't be silent. Our argument got more and more heated and I ended up shouting, so, are you telling me you approve of murder? She just stared back at me coldly and replied, 'If it means we succeed, yes I do.' I was appalled, *We*, what do you mean *we*? Are you saying you're a member of the Brigate Rosse?

She didn't need to answer; I could see from the defiant look in her eyes that she was. Before I had a chance to say anything more, she ordered me to leave and never come back. In a state of shock, I obeyed and walked out of the flat.

I couldn't believe what was happening. My finals were over, but instead of celebrating with the person I loved, I spent the rest of the day and much of the night walking around the city in a daze. I'd already arranged to vacate my digs the next day, but I couldn't face going home. In the morning I phoned my mother and told her that I'd been offered the chance of working for a year in a vineyard in France and was leaving immediately. It was the only excuse I could come up with for not going back. I tried to convince her that it was a great opportunity, but she was very upset that I wasn't coming home. She passed the phone to my father whose reaction was a thousand times worse than I'd imagined it would be. He was beside himself with rage and wasn't prepared to discuss it. He gave me an ultimatum, I should either come home straight away or not bother to come back at all. My answer was to slam down the phone.

The one-day rail strike was over, so I took a train to Milan and then another to Menton, just over the border in France. For a while I bummed around the South of France working in bars or washing dishes in restaurants, and gradually made my way up to the Bordeaux region in time for the harvest.

I did manage to get a job in a vineyard. It was hard work, but the food good, the wine plentiful and there was a party every night. I did everything I could to forget Silvana, but every night when I fell into my bed, she would fill my thoughts. I used to lie there trying to decide if I could ever accept her politics and what she was prepared to do for them."

"You never felt that you should write or go back to talk it all through with her?"

"No, I did nothing, she had sent me away, after all. I'm ashamed to say that I was too proud, too stubborn, just like my father, but, eventually, I came to accept that I still loved her and didn't want a life without her. I had to find out how she really felt about me and whether there was any chance of our having a future together, so I began to write her a series of long, rambling letters. I told her where I was and what I was doing; I told her I loved her and begged her to write back to me. When she didn't respond, I thought that she might have changed flats, so tried writing to her care of the university, but I heard nothing from her. I became so angry about her ignoring me that I vowed again to forget her. I never could, of course."

He sighs and his shoulders drop. He's exhausted.

Alice doesn't know what to say. She sits quietly looking at him for a while, then has to ask, "But that isn't the end, surely?"

"No it's not. After the grape-picking work dried up, I hitchhiked to Paris and got a job as a waiter in an Italian trattoria. I enjoyed exploring the city and learning the language properly. It's also where I improved my English, strangely enough. I shared a flat with two other waiters from the trattoria and, one morning in the January of 1982, one of them burst into my room to ask me if I'd heard about what had happened in Padova. It was all over the newspapers and radio that Italian police had raided a flat and rescued the American NATO general who'd been kidnapped in Verona the previous month. Apparently, a number of Brigate Rosse members had been arrested.

Of course, I thought of Silvana immediately. If the Brigate Rosse had been holding him in Padova, had she been involved? Had she been caught? I bought every newspaper I could and listened to every news bulletin, but they never mentioned the names of the people involved."

"Did you try to contact Silvana?"

"Yes. There wasn't a phone at the flat, so I rang the university. They told me that she wasn't a member of the faculty anymore."

"Did you stay on in Paris?"

"No, I went back home. I contacted all my old university friends to try to find out if they had any news of Silvana. They were curious about why I was interested in her, of course, so I confessed to having had a 'little romance' with her before I went away and said that I wanted to get back in touch with her. No-one could tell me anything; it seemed she'd disappeared. I went back to the university and asked for an appointment with the head of Silvana's Faculty. When I eventually managed to see him, all he'd say was that she no longer worked for the university and they had no contact details for her.

I spent endless hours wondering what had happened to her. Had she been involved in the Dozier affair in some way? Could I have stopped that happening if I'd stayed in Padova? And, however much I loved her, would I ever be able to accept her involvement with the Brigate Rosse? The sense of loss and guilt was unbearable. In the end I resolved to try to get on with my life. I decided that I must block out every thought of Silvana - after all, she could have found me if she'd loved me I kept telling myself - and vowed never to fall in love again. And I haven't, but I've never managed to forget Silvana either.

It might be difficult for you to believe, Alice, but I managed to convince myself that I hadn't let what happened affect me, or the way I've lived my life and it's only recently that I've begun to understand the impact my behaviour has on my relationship with Marco. Since he's had the girls there have been several occasions when he's tried to ask me questions about why I've never found someone to share my life with, but I've always made some silly joke to avoid telling him the truth."

"Are you ready to speak to him now? He's such a genuine and gentle person. I'm sure he'll understand."

"Yes, I think I probably am. I feel fate has taken a hand in my destiny, Alice. First you find the camera my father gave me. Then, Marco meets you and invites you to our home and, finally, you show me the pictures I took of the love of my life on our last day together. I confess everything stopped for me when I saw her face and my immediate reaction was to get as far away from you and the photos as quickly as I could.

Slowly, in the days following your visit, I realised that I had to make one last attempt to resolve the mystery of what happened to Silvana and why she had never answered my letters. I spent many, many hours searching on-line for any new information about the Dozier rescue and what had happened to the BR members involved. It turns out that four were sent to prison, but there was no mention of Silvana anywhere. The only other thing of interest I was able to discover for the day Dozier was rescued was a short article in *La Republica* about an accident involving a police car.

After exhausting the internet, I decided that my last hope was to try to contact the old head of the Faculty whom I'd spoken to all those years ago, one last time, because I'd always felt that he hadn't been entirely truthful with me. He's in his nineties now and still gives the occasional lecture, so it was relatively easy to make contact with him. I met him at his home and his first words to me were:

'I wondered if you'd ever come back. You've left it long enough, my boy! Take a seat and I'll tell you everything. So many years have passed.

Signorina Rossi's very extreme views had made her a person of interest to the anti-terrorism branch of the *polizia* and they had been keeping a watch on her and her friends for some time. It suited them for her to continue in her post at the university, rather than going underground, and so we were asked to allow her to continue teaching. When Dozier was rescued, they also captured the BR terrorist who'd been left to guard the general and, with his help, they arrested most the others directly involved. It seems that Silvana had been given the job of waiting nearby in a back-up car in case anything went wrong. When anti-terrorist police began to swarm around the apartment block and it was obvious that there was nothing she could do, she had tried to get away. Sadly, she lost control of her car, and crashed into one of the many police cars rushing to the scene. What a banal ending to her life....'

I asked him why there had been no mention of Silvana's involvement in the accident in any of the newspapers. He told me that the police were happy to pretend that it was just an ordinary road accident because they'd acted illegally in the way they had kept her under surveillance. And, as far as the University was concerned, they were anxious to avoid the bad press they would get if it was discovered that that they had employed a professor who was a BR member. Fortunately Silvana had no surviving family who might cause problems by asking awkward questions, so the university was able to arrange for her to be buried quietly alongside her parents in the Cimitero di Opicina in Trieste."

THE CAMERA

Epilogue
Six Months Later

Alice has been fizzing with excitement since she woke up this morning, but, suddenly she begins to worry. It had seemed such a brilliant idea when she'd suggested it, but what if it turned out to be a disaster? When she walks into the terminal, a quick glance at the arrivals board tells her that the flight is due to land on time. A grappa would definitely steady her nerves, but she's driving, so will have to make do with an *espresso*. As she waits for her coffee, she takes a deep breath, filling her lungs to bursting point. After a count of seven, she exhales slowly through her mouth and repeats the process a few times, relieved to find that she feels a little calmer. Her espresso, when it arrives, tastes good and she's just finishing scooping up the *crema* at the bottom of her cup when the public address system announces that the flight from London is about to arrive.

Many of the people in the bar seem to be making their way towards the floor length windows overlooking the runway, so Alice decides to join them. Everyone watches with a rising sense of excitement as the aircraft taxies slowly towards the terminal. Ground staff wearing smart blue overalls the exact shade of the *Azzuri,* (the Italian football squad), teamed with trendy aviator sunglasses, begin to roll a set of boarding stairs towards the plane. They had all looked equally stylish when she'd arrived yesterday, pretending she was a 1950s film star as she'd made her way down the stairs and onto the tarmac. It had been hard to stifle the urge to smile at some imaginary *paparazzi.*

Passengers begin to disembark and it seems to take an age before Georgie emerges, closely followed by Freya and Rob. They look happy and Alice finds herself waving. Somehow, Rob spots her and they all wave back. It's all going to be OK.

***

The drive goes well, with Alice doing her best to answer all the questions her friends have about the places they pass. She's grateful for the distraction, because she's beginning to feel nervous again. But, again, there's no need to worry because as soon as they arrive Luca, Valeria, Marco and the girls pour out of the house and are incredibly welcoming. Everyone is ushered out onto the terrace where antipasti, glasses and two ice buckets containing bottles of *Tenuta Grauner* wines are waiting.

Freya immediately begins to exclaim loudly about how 'FABULOUS' everything is, Georgie kneels to chat to the girls and Rob finds a seat at the table, where he eagerly surveys the food on offer. His appetite has returned, as has his positive outlook on life, thank goodness.

Luca busies himself with opening the wine, but still

manages to catch Alice's eye and smile broadly back at her. She should get on and hand out the glasses Luca is filling. First she delivers a glass to Rob and, seeing that Marco has already taken care of Georgie and Valeria, picks up a couple of glasses for herself and Freya.

"Here we are sweetie, your first taste of Grauner wine."

"Thanks. My God, Alice, this place is amazing. Absolutely idyllic!" Grabbing Alice's arm she leans conspiratorially towards her, "Why don't we go and have a little talk?"

Alice motions to Luca that they are popping outside. He pauses his conversation with Rob for a moment, smiles and nods.

"Now isn't the time I know, but you've got to fill me on *everything* that's been happening and on how things are going. Obviously, I've only just met him, but Luca seems perfect and I haven't failed to notice how he looks at you. I've been thinking... "

"Oh no. Ever since I've known you, I've dreaded hearing those words. They usually mean that you are going to try to force me to do something completely outside my comfort zone."

"Well darling, you never were what anyone would call a 'wild child' were you? You always needed a little push! But listen, *tempus* is *fugiting* and all this is too good to throw away, so, as I was trying to say before I was so rudely interrupted, you can work anywhere - you're always saying that - so why don't you arrange to rent out your house for say, six months, and give things a go with Luca, here?"

The sound of steel tinkling on glass catches everyone's attention. It looks as if Luca is going to say a few words, so they move back inside.

"I'd like to take the opportunity to welcome you all to our

home. We are delighted to meet you because we have heard so much about you all from Alice and we hope, very much, that you will enjoy your stay with us. *Benvenuti*, welcome!"

As food is enjoyed and glasses refilled, everyone chats happily. Although Alice doesn't want to break things up, once the second bottle of Pinot Grigio has been upended in its ice bucket, she suggests that, perhaps, her friends might like to unpack and have a rest before dinner which is being hosted by Luca at the restaurant later.

Whilst they'd been enjoying their second bottle of wine, Marco had kindly looked after everyone's luggage, so Luca ushers Rob towards the door, "Will you join me in showing your friends where they will be staying, Alice? He and Rob then fall into step in front, with the girls following close behind. In as quiet a whisper as she can manage, which isn't quiet at all, Freya shares her thoughts on Luca once again.

"He's absolutely gorgeous, Alice. You *must* hold on to him!"

Georgie groans, "Oh mum, shut up, Luca must be able to hear you!"She's right because, at moment, Rob turns around to look at them with an amused raised eyebrow stare. Suitably chastened, Freya walks on in silence.

***

As Alice changes for dinner she reflects on all that has happened in the last six months. Once Luca had finished his story, neither of them had spoken for a long time. As she sat there she had thought about how painful it must have been for him to finally discover what had happened to Silvana all those years ago and had experienced a huge surge of affection for him.

Eventually, he had turned to her, "Thank you for listening."

Afraid that anything she said at that moment would sound trite or clichéd, she had smiled and taken his hand. They had arranged to meet the following day for an early supper before Luca returned home and had enjoyed the meal because Luca's previous restraint had disappeared. They had talked and laughed nonstop. Since then, they had visited each other for weekends and their friendship had deepened.

On his next visit to London, Luca had told her the final part of his story. "When I got back from London, I went straight to the cemetery in Trieste. It was deserted, apart from an old man sweeping up the fallen leaves. I explained to him that I was looking for a Silvana Rossi who had been buried in a family plot in 1982. As soon as I mentioned her name, the man's eyes lit up.

'Ah yes, the daughter of Cinzia and Demostene Rossi! They were famous in their time in this area, you know. Brave partisans. You'll find them in *campo* H over there, in the shelter of the wall. Are you family? I only ask because the payment on the plot runs out in six months - you'll find a small notice when you get there.'

What I found was a stark, grey marble rectangle set into the earth. No epitaph or dates, just the words

ROSSI
Cinzia, Demostene, Silvana.

carved into the stone.

The next day I paid to secure the plot for ninety nine years. The thought of Silvana's bones ending up in the communal ossuary was too horrible to imagine. I've made my peace with

Silvana, Alice. I've also spoken, at length, to Marco, Valeria and even to my brother, all of whom have extremely understanding. I can't change the past, but I'm determined not to let it ruin my future."

***

Alice finishes applying her lipstick, closes the door and walks downstairs.

"You look nice!" Valeria calls out as she clips a pretty slide into Antonella's hair."Luca and Marco are already down at the restaurant; would you like to walk down with me and the girls?"

"Thank you Valeria, but I promised to show my friends the way, so I'll meet you there."

Walking through the little woodland, Alice pauses to savour the moment. Here she is, surrounded by the people she loves and about to enjoy what she knows will be a wonderful evening. Georgie is calling her name...

ACKNOWLEDGMENTS

Like many people, I have dreamed of writing a novel but have never had the self belief to make it happen. The push I needed was provided by Ian, who challenged me to take part in NaNoWriMo (National Novel Writing Month) in November 2018. Without this spur and the motivation NaNoWriMo provides, my story would never have been written. I also want to thank my family and friends for their support and encouragement during the whole process.

ABOUT THE AUTHOR

Valentina Church was born in South Wales of Welsh and Italian parents. She grew up there, visiting Italy each summer to spend time with her grandparents. After living in London for many years she recently moved and has now made her home in the Chiltern Hills of Buckinghamshire.

Printed in Poland
by Amazon Fulfillment
Poland Sp. z o.o., Wrocław